I0638154

Killing Yourself to Survive

STORIES

Killing Yourself to Survive

STORIES

David Corbett

A MYSTERIOUSPRESS.COM BOOK

OPEN ROAD

INTEGRATED MEDIA

NEW YORK

Contents

Pretty Little Parasite

ONE HAND ON HER HIP, the other lofting her cocktail tray, Sam Pitney scanned the gaming floor from the Roundup's mezzanine, dressed in her cowgirl outfit and fresh from a bracing toot in the ladies. Stream-of-nothingness mode, mid-shift, slow night, only the blow keeping her vertical—and she had this odd craving for some stir-fry—she stared out at the flagging crowd and manically finger-brushed the outcrop of blond bangs showing beneath her tipped-back hat.

Maybe it was seeing her own reflection fragmented in dozens of angled mirrors to the left and right and even overhead, or the sight of the usual trudge of losers wandering the noisy maze-like neon, clutching change buckets, chip trays, chain-smoking (still legal, this was the '80s), hoping for one good score to recoup a little dignity—whatever the reason, she found herself revisiting a TV program from a few nights back, about Auschwitz, Dachau, one of those places. Men and women and children and even poor helpless babies cradled by their mothers, stripped naked then marched into giant shower rooms, only to notice too late—doors slamming, bolts thrown, gas soon hissing from the showerheads: a smell like almonds, the voice on the program said.

Sam found herself wondering—no particular reason—what it would be like if the doors to the casino suddenly rumbled shut, trapping everybody inside.

For a moment or two, she supposed, no one would even notice, gamblers being what they are. But soon enough word would ripple through the crowd, especially when the fire sprinklers in the ceiling started to mist. Even then, people would be puzzled and vaguely put out but not frightened, not until somebody nearby started gagging, buckled over, a barking cough, the scalding phlegm, a slime of blood in the palm.

Then panic, the rush for the doors. Screaming. Animal terror.

Sam wondered where she'd get found when they finally reopened the doors to deal with the dead. Would she be one of those with bloody nails or, worse, fingers worn down to gory bone, having tried to claw her way past so many others to sniff at an air vent, a door crack, ready to kill for just one more breath? Or would she be one of the others, one of those they found alone, having caught on quick and then surrendered, figuring she was screwed, knowing it in the pit of her soul, curled up on the floor, waiting for God or Mommy or Satan or who-the-fuck-ever to put an end to the tedious phony bullshit, the nerves and the worry and the always being tired, the lonely winner-takes-all, the grand American nothing ...

"Could I possibly have another whiskey and ginger, luv?"

Sam snapped toward the voice—the accent crisply British once, now blurred by years among the Vegas gypsies. It came from a face of singular unlucky pallor: high brow with a froth of chestnut hair, flat bloodless lips, no chin to speak of. The Roundup sat just east of Las Vegas Boulevard on Fremont, closer to the LVPD Metro tower than the tonier downtown houses— the Four Queens, the Golden Nugget—catering to whoever showed up first and stayed longest, cheap tourists mostly, dopes who'd just stumbled out of the drunk tank and felt lucky (figure that one out)—or, most inexplicably, locals, the transplant kind especially, the ones who went on and on about old Las Vegas, which meant goofs like this bird. What was his name? Harvey, Harold, something with an H. He taught at UNLV if she remembered right, came here three nights a week at least, often more, said it was for the nostalgia ...

"You are on the clock, my dear, am I right?"

She gazed into his soupy green eyes. Centuries of inbreeding. Hail, Brittania.

"I'm pregnant," she said.

COME MIDNIGHT SHE BEGAN looking for Mike, and found him off by himself in the dollar slots, an odd little nook where there were fewer mirrors, and the eye in the sky had a less than perfect angle (he thought of these things). He wore white linen slacks, a pastel tee, the sleeves of his sport jacket rolled up. All Sonny Crockett, the dick.

"Hey," she said, coming up.

He shot her a vaguely proprietary smile. His eyes looked wrecked but his hair was flawless. He said, "The usual?"

"No, weekend coming up. Make it two."

The smile thawed, till it seemed almost friendly. "Double your pleasure."

She clipped off to the bar, ordered a Stoli rocks twist, discreetly assembling the twelve twenties on her tray in a tight thin stack. The casino's monotonous racket jangled all around, same at midnight as happy hour—the eternal now, she thought, Vegas time.

Returning to where he sat, she bowed at the waist, so he could reach the tray. He carefully set a five down, under which he'd tucked two wax-paper bindles. Then he collected the twelve twenties off her tray, as though they were his change, and she remembered the last time they were together, in her bed, the faraway look he got afterwards, not wanting to be touched, the kind of thing guys did when they'd had enough of you.

"Whoever you get this from," she said, "I want to meet him."

From the look on his face, you would've thought she'd asked for the money back. "Come again?"

"You heard me."

He cocked his head. The hair didn't budge. "I'm not sure I like your attitude."

She broke the news. In the span of only a second or so, his expression went from stunned to deflated to distinctly pissed, then: "You saying it's mine?"

She rolled her eyes. "No. An angel came to me."

"Don't get smart."

"Oh, smart's exactly what I'm going for, believe me."

"Okay then, take care of it."

With those few words, she got a picture of his ideal woman—a collie in heat, basically, but with fewer scruples. Lay out a few lines, bend her over the sofa, splay her ass—then a few weeks later, tell her to *take care of it.*

"Sorry," she said. "Not gonna happen."

He chuckled acidly. "Since when are you maternal?"

"Don't think you know me. We fucked, that's it."

"You're shaking me down."

"I'm filling you in. But yeah, I could make this a problem. Instead, I'm trying to do the right thing. For everybody. But I'm not gonna be able to work here much longer, understand? This ain't about you, it's about money. Introduce me to your guy."

He thought about it, and as he did his lips curled into a grin. The eyes were still scared though. "Who says it's a guy?"

A twinge lit up her lower back. Get used to it, she thought. "Don't push me, Mike. I'm a woman scorned, with a muffin in the oven." She did a quick pivot and headed off. Over her shoulder, she added, "I'm off at two. Set it up."

IT DIDN'T HAPPEN that night, as it turned out, and that didn't surprise her. What did surprise her was that it happened only two nights later, and she didn't have to hound him half as bad as she'd expected—more surprising still, he hadn't been jiving: It really wasn't a guy.

Her name was Claudia, a Cuban, maybe fifty, could pass for forty, calm dark eyes that waxed and waned between cordial welcome and cold appraisal—a tiny woman, raven-black hair coiled tight into a long braid, body as sleek as a razor, sheathed in a simple black dress. She lived in one of the newer condos at the other end of Fremont, near Sahara, where it turned into Boulder Highway.

Claudia showed them in, dead-bolted the door, offered a cool muscular hand to Sam with a nod, then gestured everyone into the living room: suede furniture, Navajo rugs, ferns. Two fluffed and imperial Persian cats nestled near the window on matching cushions. Across the room, a mobile of tiny tin birds, dozens of them, all painted bright tropical colors, hung from the ceiling. Thing must torment the cats, Sam thought, glancing up as she tucked her skirt against her thighs.

"Like I said before," Mike began, addressing Claudia, "I think this is a bogus idea, but you said okay, so here we are."

Sam resisted an urge to storm over, take two fistfuls of that pampered hair, and rip it out by the roots. She turned to the woman. "Can we talk alone?"

"That doesn't work for me," Mike said.

With the grace of a model, Claudia slowly pivoted toward him. "I think it's for the best." For the sake of his pride, she added, "I'm sure I'll be fine."

That was that. He sulked off to the patio, the two women talked. It didn't take long for Sam to explain her situation, lay out her plan, make it clear she wasn't being flaky or impulsive. She'd thought it through—she didn't want to get even, pick off Mike's customers, nothing like that. "I don't want to hand my baby off to daycare, some stranger. I want to be there. At home."

Claudia eyed her, saying nothing, for what seemed an eternity. Don't look away, Sam told herself. Accept the scrutiny, know your role. But don't act scared.

"There are those," Claudia said finally, "who would find what you just said very peculiar." Her smile seemed a kind of warning, and yet it wasn't without warmth. "I'm sure you realize that."

"I do. But I think you understand."

It turned out she understood only too well—she had a son, Marco, eleven years old, away at boarding school in Seville. "I miss him terribly." She made a sawing motion. "Like someone cut off my arm."

"Why don't you have him here, with you?"

For the first time, Claudia looked away. Her face darkened. "Mothers make sacrifices. It's not all about staying home with the baby."

Sam felt backward, foolish, hopelessly American. Behold the future, she thought, ten years down the road, doing this, and your kid is where? In the corner of her eye, she saw one of the cats rise sleepily and arch its back. Out on the patio, Mike sat in the moonlight, a sudden red glow as he dragged on his cigarette.

Claudia steered the conversation to terms: Sam would start off buying ounces at two thousand dollars each, which she would divide into grams and eightballs for sale. If things went well, she could move up to a QP—quarter pound—at $7800, build her clientele. She might well plateau at that point, many did. If she was ambitious, though, she could move up to an elbow—for "lb," meaning a pound—with the tacit agreement she would not interfere with Claudia's wholesale trade.

"I want you to look me in the eye, Samantha. Good. Do not confuse my sympathy for weakness. I'm generous by nature. That doesn't mean I'm stupid. I have men who take care of certain matters for me, men not at all like our friend out there." She nodded toward Mike all alone on the moonlit patio. "These men, you will never meet them unless it comes to that. And if it does, the time will have passed for you to say or do anything to help yourself. I trust I'm clear."

THE FIRST AND oddest thing? She lost five pounds. God, she thought, what have I done? She checked her sheets for blood, then ran to Valley Medical, no appointment, demanded to see her ob-gyn. The receptionist—sagging desert face, kinky gray perm—shot her one of those knowing, gallingly sympathetic looks you never really live down.

"Your body thinks you've got a parasite, dear," the woman said. "Just keep eating."

She did, and she stunned herself, how quickly her habits turned healthy. No more coke, ditto booze—instead a passion for bananas (craving potassium), an obsession with yogurt (good for bone mass, the immune system, the intestinal lining), a sudden interest in whole grains (to keep her regular), citrus (for iron absorption), even liver (prevent anemia). She took to grazing, little meals here and there, to keep the nausea at bay, and when her appetite craved more she turned to her newfound favorite: stir-fry.

She continued working for three months, time enough to groom a clientele—fellow casino rats (her old quitting-time buddies, basically, and their buddies), a few select customers from the Roundup (including, strangely enough, Harry the homely Brit, who came from Manchester, she learned, taught mechanical engineering, vacationed in Cabo most winters, not half the schmuck she'd pegged him for), plus a few locals she decided to trust (the girls at Diva's Hair-and-Nail, the boys at Monte Carlo Tanning Salon, a locksmith named Nick Perino, had a shop just up Fremont Street, total card, used to host a midnight movie show in town)—all of this happening in the shadow of the Metro tower on Stewart Street, all those cops just four blocks away.

Business was brisk. She got current on her bills, socked away a few grand. At sixteen weeks her stomach popped out, like she'd suddenly inflated, and that was the end of cocktail shift. Sam bid it goodbye with no regrets, the red pleated dress, the cowboy hat, the tasseled boots. From that point forward, she conducted business where she pleased, permitting a trustworthy inner circle to come to her place, the others she met out and about, merrily invisible in her maternity clothes.

The birth was strangely easy, two-hour labor, a snap by most standards, and Sam shed twenty pounds before heading home. The best thing about seeing it go was no longer having to endure strangers—older women especially, riding with her in elevators or standing in line at the store—who would notice the tight globe of her late-term belly and instinctively reach out, stroke the shuddering roundness, cooing in a helpless, mysterious, covetous way that almost rekindled Sam's childhood fear of witches.

As for the last of the weight gain, it all seemed to settle in her chest—first time in her life, she had cleavage. This little girl's been good to you all over, Sam thought—her skin shone, her eyes glowed, she looked happy. Guys seemed to notice, clients especially, but she made sure to keep it all professional: So much as hint at sex with coke in the room, next thing you knew the guy'd be eyeing your muff like it was veal.

Besides, the interest on her end had vanished. Curiously, that didn't faze her. Whatever it was she'd once craved from her lovers she now got from Natalie, feeling it strongest when she nursed, enjoying something she'd secretly thought didn't exist— the kind of fierce unshakeable oneness she'd always thought was just Hollywood. Now she knew better. The crimped pink face, the curled doughy hands, the wispy black strands of impossibly fine hair: "Look at you," she'd whisper, over and over and over.

By the end of two months, she'd pitched all her old clothes, not just the maternity duds. Some old habits got the heave-ho as well: the trashy attitude, slutty speech, negative turns of mind. Nor would the apartment do anymore—too dark, too small, too blah. The little one deserves better, she told herself, as does her mother. Besides, maybe someone had noticed all the in and out, the visitors night and day. Half paranoia, half healthy faith in who she'd become, she upscaled to a three-bedroom out on Boulder Highway, furnished it in suede, added ferns. She bought two cats.

NICK PERINO SAT ALONE in an interview room in the Stewart Street Tower—dull yellow walls, scuffed black linoleum, humming fluorescent light—tapping his thumbs together and cracking his neck as he waited. Finally the door opened, and he tried to muster some advantage, assert control, by challenging the man who entered with, "I don't know you."

The newcomer ignored him, tossing a manila folder onto the table as he drew back his chair to sit. He was in his thirties, shaggy hair, wiry build, dressed in a Runnin' Rebels T-shirt and faded jeans. Something about him said one-time jock. Something else said unmitigated prick. Looking bored, he opened the file, began leafing through the pages, sipping from a paper cup of steaming black coffee so vile Nick could smell it across the table.

Nick said, "I'm used to dealing with Detective Naughton."

The guy sniffed, chuckling at something he read, suntanned

laugh lines fanning out at his eyes. "Yeah, well, he's been rotated out to Traffic. You witness a nasty accident, Mike's your man. But that's not why you're here, is it Mr. Perry?"

"Perino."

The cop glanced up finally. His eyes were scary blue and so bloodshot they looked on fire. Another sniff. "Right. Forgive me."

"Some kind of cold you got there. Must be the air-conditioning."

"It's allergies, actually."

Nick chuckled. Allergic to sleep, maybe. "Speaking of names, you got one?"

"Thornton." He whipped back another page. "Chief calls me James, friends call me Jimmy. You can call me sir."

Nick stood up. He wasn't going to take this, not from some slacker narc half in the bag. "I came here to do you guys a favor."

Still picking through the file, Jimmy Thornton said, "Sit back down, Mr. Perry."

"Don't call me that."

"I said—sit down."

"You think you're talking to some fart-fuck asshole?"

Finally, the cop closed the file. Removing a ballpoint pen from his hip pocket, he began thumbing the plunger manically. "I know who I'm talking to. Mike paints a pretty vivid picture." He nudged the folder across the table. "Want a peek?"

Despite himself, Nick recoiled a little. "Yeah. Maybe I'll do that."

Leaning back in his chair, still clicking the pen, Jimmy Thornton said: "You first blew into town, when was it, '74? Nick Perry, *Chiller Theater*, Saturday midnight. Weaseled your way into the job, touting all this 'network experience' back east."

Nick shrugged. "Everybody lies on his resume."

"Not everybody."

"My grandfather came over from Sicily, Perino was the family name. Ellis Island, he changed it to Perry. I just changed it back."

"Yeah, but not till you went to work for Johnny T."

Nick could feel the blood drain from his face. "What are you getting at?"

The cop's smile turned poisonous. "Know what Johnny said about you? You're the only guy in Vegas ever *added* a vowel to the end of his name. Him and his brother, saw you coming at the San Genero Festival, they couldn't run the other way fast enough, even when you worked for them. Worst case of wanna-be-wiseguy they'd ever seen."

Finally, Nick sat back down. "You heard this how? Johnny doesn't, like—"

"Know you were the snitch? Can't answer that. I mean, he probably suspects."

Nick had been a CI in a state case against the Tintoretto brothers for prostitution and drugs, all run through their massage parlor out on Flamingo. Nick remained unidentified during trial, the case made on wiretaps. It seemed a wise play at the time—get down first, tell the story his way, cut a deal, before the roof caved in. He was working as the manager there, only job he could find in town after getting canned at the station—a nigger joke, pussy in the punch line, didn't know he was on the air.

"All the employees got a pass," Nick said, "not just me. Johnny couldn't know for sure unless you guys told him."

"Relax." Another punctuating sniff. "Nobody around here told him squat. We keep our promises, Mr. Perry."

Nick snorted. "Not from where I sit."

"Excuse me?" The guy leaned in. "Mike bent over backwards for you, pal. Set you up, perfect location, right downtown. Felons aren't supposed to be locksmiths."

"Most of that stuff on my sheet was out of state. And it got expunged."

A chuckle: "Now there's a word."

"Vacated, sealed, whatever."

"Because Mike took care of it. And how do you repay him?"

"I don't know what you're talking about."

"Every time business gets slow, you send that fat freak you call a nephew out to the apartments off Maryland Parkway—middle of the night, spray can of Super Glue, gum up a couple hundred locks. You can bank on at least a third of the calls, given your location—think we don't know this?"

"Who you talking to, Mike Lally over at All-Night Lock'n'Key? You wanna hammer a crook, there's your guy, not me."

"Doesn't have thirty-two grand in liens from the Tax Commission on his business, though, does he?"

Nick blanched. They already knew. They knew everything. "I got screwed by my bookkeeper. Look, I came here with information. You wanna hear it or not?"

"In exchange for getting the Tax Commission off your neck."

"Before they shut me down, yeah. That asking so much?"

Jimmy Thornton opened the manila folder to the last page, clicked his pen one final time, and prepared to write. "That depends."

SAM SAT IN THE SHADE at the playground two blocks from her apartment, listening to Nick go on. He'd just put in new locks at her apartment—she changed them every few weeks now, just being careful—and, stopping here to drop off the new keys, he'd sat down on the bench beside her, launching in, some character named Jimmy.

"He's a stand-up guy," Nick said. "Looker, too. You'll like him."

"You pitching him as a customer, or a date?"

Nick raised his hands, a coy smile, "All things are possible," inflecting the words with that *paisano* thing he fell into sometimes.

Natalie slept in her stroller, exhausted from an hour on the swings, the slide, the merry-go-round. Sam wondered about that, whether it was really good for kids to indulge that giddy instinct for dizziness. Where did it lead?

"Tell me again how you met this guy."

"He wanted a wall safe, I installed it for him."

She squinted in the sun, shaded her eyes. "What's he need a wall safe for?"

"That's not a question I ask. You want, I provide. That's business, as you well know."

She suffered him a thin smile. With the gradual expansion of her clientele—no one but referrals, but even so her base had almost doubled—she'd watched herself pulling back from people, even old friends, a protective, judicious remove. And that was lonely-making. Worse, she'd gotten used to it, and that seemed a kind of living death. The only grace was Natalie, but even there, the oneness she'd felt those first incredible months, that had changed as well. She still adored the girl, loved her to pieces, that wasn't the issue. Little girls grow up, their mothers get lonely, where's the mystery? She just hadn't expected it to start so soon.

"He's a contractor," Nick went on, "works down in Henderson. I saw the blueprints and, you know, stuff in his place when I was there. Look, you don't need the trade, forget about it. But I thought, I dunno, maybe you'd like the guy."

"I don't need to like him."

"I meant 'like' as in 'do business'."

Sam checked the stroller. Natalie had her thumb in her mouth, eyes closed, her free hand balled into a fist beneath her chin.

"You know how this works," Sam said. "He causes trouble, anything at all—I mean this, Nick—anything at all comes back at me, it's on you, not just him."

THEY MET AT THE Elephant Walk, and it turned out Nick was right, the guy turned heads—an easy grace, cowboy shoulders, lady-killer smile. He ordered Johnny Walker Black with a splash, and Sam remembered, from her days working cocktail, judging men by their drinks. He'd ordered wisely. And yet there were signs—a jitter in the hands, a slight head tic, the red in those killer blue eyes. Then again, if she worried that her customers looked like users, who would she sell to?

"Nick says you're a contractor."

He shook his head. "Project manager."

"There's a difference?"

"Sometimes. Not often enough." He laughed and the laugh was self-effacing, one more winning trait. "I buy materials, hire the subs, make sure the bonds are current and we're all on time. But the contractor's the one with his license on the line."

"Sounds demanding."

"Everything's demanding. If it means anything."

She liked that answer. "And to relax, you … ?"

He shrugged. "I've got a bike, a Triumph, old bandit 350, gathering dust in my garage." Another self-effacing smile. "Amazing how boring you can sound when stuff like that comes out."

Not boring, she thought. Just normal. "Ever been married?"

A fierce little jolt shot through him. "Once. Yeah. High school sweetheart kind of thing. Didn't work out."

She got the hint, and steered the conversation off in a different direction. They talked about Nick, the stories they'd heard him tell about his TV days, wondering which ones to believe. Sam asked about how the two men had met, got the same story she'd heard from Nick, embellished a little, not too much. Things were, basically, checking out.

Sensing it was time, she signaled the bartender to settle up. "Well, it's been very nice meeting you, Jimmy. I have to get home. The sitter awaits, with the princess."

"Nick told me. Natalie, right? Have any pictures?"

She liked it when men asked to see pictures. It said something. She took out her wallet, opened it to the snapshots.

"How old?"

"Fifteen months. Just."

"She's got her mother's eyes."

"She's got more than that, sadly."

"No. Good for her." He returned her wallet, hand not trembling now. Maybe it was the scotch, maybe the conversation. "She's a beauty. Changed your life, I'll bet."

Yes, Sam thought, that she has. Maybe we'll talk about that sometime. Next time. "Have kids?"

Very subtly, his eyes hazed. "Me? No. Didn't get that far, which is probably for the best. Got some nephews and nieces, that's it for now."

"Uncle Jimmy."

He rattled the ice in his glass, traveled somewhere with his thoughts. "I like kids. Want kids. My turn'll come." Then, brightening suddenly: "I'd be up for a play date some time, with Natalie. I mean, if that doesn't sound too weird."

THAT'S HOW IT STARTED, same playground near the apartment. And he hadn't lied, he hit it off with Natalie at first sight—stunning, really. He was a natural, carrying her on his shoulders to the park, guiding her up the stairs to the slide, taking it easy on the swing. He had Sam cradle her in her lap on the merry-go-round, spun them both around in the sun-streaked shade. Natalie shrieked, Sam laughed; it was that kind of afternoon.

They brought Natalie home, put her down for her nap, then sat on the porch with drinks—the usual for him, Chablis for her. The sun beat down on the freshly watered lawn, a hot desert wind rustling the leaves of the imported elm trees.

Surveying the grounds, he said, "Nice place. Mind if I ask your monthly nut?"

"Frankly?"

He chuckled. "Sorry. Professional curiosity. I was just doing the math in my head, tallying costs, wondering what kind of return the developer's getting."

She smiled wanly. "I don't like to think about it." That seemed as good a way as any to change the subject. "So, Nick says you wanted to ask me something."

Suddenly, he looked awkward, a hint of a blush. It suited him.

"Well, yeah. I suppose … You know. Sometimes …" He gestured vaguely.

She said, "Don't make me say it for you."

He cleared his throat. "I could maybe use an eightball. Sure."

There, she thought. Was that so hard? "Let's say a gram. I don't know you."

"How about two?"

It was still below the threshold for a special felony, which an eightball, at 3.5 grams, wasn't. "Two-forty, no credit."

"No friend-of-a-friend discount?"

"Nick told you there would be?"

"No, I just—"

"There isn't. There won't be."

He raised his hands, surrender. "Okay." He reached into his hip pocket for his wallet. "Mind if I take a shot while I'm here?"

She collected her glass, rose from her chair. "I'd prefer it, actually. Come on inside." She gestured for him to have a seat on the couch, disappeared into her bedroom, and returned with the coke, delivering the two grams with a mirror, a razor blade, a straw. As always, a stranger in the house, one of the cats sat in the corner, blinking. The other hid. Sam watched as Jimmy chopped up the lines, an old hand. He hoovered the first, offered her the mirror. She declined. He leaned back down, finished up, tugged at his nose.

"That's nice," he said, collecting the last few grains on his finger, rubbing it into his gums. When his hand came away, it left a smile behind. "I'm guessing Mannitol. I mean, you've got it around, right?"

Sam took a sip of her wine. He was referring to a baby laxative commonly used as a cutting agent. Coolly, she said, "Let a girl have her secrets."

He nodded. "Sorry. That was out of line."

"Don't worry about it." She toddled her glass. "So—will there be anything else?"

She didn't mean to sound coy, but even so she inwardly cringed as she heard the words out loud. The way he looked at her, it was clear he was trying to decipher the signal. And maybe, on some level, she really did mean something.

"No," he said. "I think that's it. Mind if I take one last look before I leave?"

And so that's how they wrapped it up, standing in the doorway to Natalie's room, watching her sleep.

"Such a pretty little creature," he whispered. "Gotta confess, I'm jealous."

BACK IN HIS CAR, Jimmy horned the rest of the first gram, then drove to the Roundup, a little recon, putting faces to names, customers of Sam's that Nick had told him about: card dealers, waitresses, a gambler named Harry Thune, homely Brit, the usual ghastly teeth. After that, he drove to the strip mall on Charleston where the undercover unit had its off-site location, an anonymous set of offices with blinds drawn, a sign on the door reading "Halliwell Partners, Ltd." He logged in, parked at his desk, and wrote up his report: the purchase of one gram Cocaine HCL, field tested positive with Scott reagent—blue, pink, then blue with pink separation in successive ampoules after agitation—said gram supplied by Samantha Pitney, White Female Adult. He invented an encounter far more fitting with department guidelines than the one that had taken place, wrote it out, signed it, then drove to Metro tower, walked in the back entrance, and delivered the report to his sergeant, an old hand named Becker, who sent Jimmy on to log the gram into evidence. Jimmy said hey to the secretaries on his way through the building, went back to his car, moved $120 from his personal wallet to his buy wallet to cover the gram he'd pilfered, then planned his next step.

The following two buys were the same, two grams, and she seemed to grow more comfortable. He got bumped up to an eightball, and not long after that he rose to two. He always took a taste right there at the apartment, while they were talking, one of the perks of the job. Later, he'd either log it in as-is, claiming the shortage had been used for field-testing, or he'd pocket the light one, chop it up into grams, then drive to Henderson—or, on weekends, all the way to Laughlin—work the bars, a little business for himself, cover his costs, a few like minds, deputies he knew.

He found himself oddly divided on Sam. You could see she'd tried to cultivate an aura: the wry feminine reserve, the earth tones, all the talk about yoga and studying for her real estate license. Maybe it was motherhood, all that scrubbed civility, trying to be somebody. Then again, maybe it was cokehead pretense. Regardless, little things tripped her up, those selfless moments, more and more frequent, when she let him see behind the mask. Trouble was, from what he could tell, the mask had more to offer.

He'd nailed a witness or two in his time, never a smooth move, but nothing compared to bedding a suspect. As fluid as things had become morally since he'd started working undercover, he'd never lost track of that particular red line. That didn't mean he didn't entertain the thought—throwing her over his shoulder, carrying her into her room, dropping her onto the bed, watching her hair unfurl from the soft thudding impact. Would she try to fight him off—no, that would just be part of the dance. Soon enough she'd draw him down, a winsome smile, hands clasped behind his neck, a few quick nibbles in her kiss, now and then a good firm bite. And was she one of those who showed you around the castle—how hard to pinch the nipples, how many fingers inside, the hand clasped across her mouth as she came—or would she want you to find all that out for yourself? Playing coy, demure, wanting you to take command, maybe even scare her. How deep would she like it, how slow, how rough? Would she come in rolling pulses, or one big back-arching slam?

Then again, of course, there was Natalie. Truth be told, she was the one who'd stolen his heart. And it was clear her poor deluded mother loved her, but love's not enough—never is, never has been. He remembered Sam asking, in their first face-to-face, about his marriage, about kids. You're not a cop till your first divorce, he thought, go through the custody horseshit. Lose. Bobby was his name. Seven years old now. Somewhere.

When he found himself thinking like that, he also found himself developing a mean thirst. And when he drank, he liked a whiff, to steady the ride, ice it. And so soon he'd be back at Ms. Pitney's door, repeating the whole sad process, telling himself the same wrong stories, wanting everything he had no right to.

SIX WEEKS INTO THINGS, he asked, "What made you get into this business anyway?"

She was sitting on the sofa, legs tucked beneath her, wearing a new perfume. From the look on her face, you would've thought he'd spat on the floor. "No offense, but that came out sounding ugly."

He razored away at three chalky lines. "Didn't mean it that way. Sorry."

She thought about it for a moment, searching the ceiling with her eyes. "The truth? I wanted to be a stay-at-home mom."

He had to check himself, to keep from laughing, and yet he could see it. So her, thinking that way. "Why not marry the father?"

Again, she took her time before answering, but this time she didn't scour the ceiling, she gazed into his face. Admittedly, he was a little ragged: His mouth was dry, his eyes were jigging up and down, his pupils were bloated. And his hands, yeah, a mild but noticeable case of the shakes.

"Some men are meant to be fathers," she said. "Some men aren't."

SAM LET ONE OF Claudia's Persians settle in her lap, pressing her skirt with its paws. The other cat lay in its usual spot, on the cushion by the window, lolling in the sun. Natalie sat in her stroller, gumming an apple slice, while Claudia attended her ferns, using a tea kettle for a watering can.

"I usually charge thirty, which is already low, but I'd trim a little more, say twenty-eight." She was talking in thousands of dollars, the price for a pound—or an elbow, in the parlance.

"That's still a little steep for me."

"You could cut your visits here by half. More."

"Is that a problem?" Secretly, Sam loved coming here. She thought of it as Visiting Mother.

Over her shoulder, Claudia said, "You know what I mean."

"Maybe I'll ratchet up another QP. I don't want any more

than that in the house." Claudia bent to reach a pot on the floor. "The point is to get it *out* of the house."

Well duh, Sam thought, feeling judged, a headache looming like a thunderhead just behind her eyes. She was getting them more and more. "There's something else I'd like to talk over, actually. It's about Natalie."

Claudia stopped short. "Is something wrong?"

"No. Not yet. I mean, there's nothing to worry about. But if anything ever happened to me, I don't know who would take care of her."

A disagreeable expression crossed Claudia's face, part disdain, part calculation, part suspicion. "You have family."

"Not local. And not that I trust, frankly."

"What exactly are you asking?"

"I was wondering if she could stay with you. If anything ever happened, I mean."

Claudia put the tea kettle down and came over to a nearby chair, crossing her legs as she sat. "Have you noticed any cars following you lately?"

"It's not like that."

"Any new neighbors?"

"That wasn't what I meant. I meant if I got sick, or was in a car accident." She glanced over at Natalie. The apple slice was nubby and brown, and both it and her fingers were glazed with saliva.

Claudia said, "I couldn't just walk in, take your child. Good Lord."

Her voice rippled, a blast of heat. Sam said, "I'm sorry, I didn't mean—"

"A dozen agencies would be involved, imagine the questions." She rose from her chair, straightened her skirt, shot a toxic glance at Natalie that said: Your mother can't protect you. "Now what quantity are you here for? I have things to do."

SERGEANT BECKER CALLED Jimmy in, told him to close the door. He was a big man, the kind who could lord over you even sitting down. "This Pitney thing, I've gone over the reports." He picked up a pencil, drummed it against his blotter. "Your buys are light."

He stared into Jimmy's whirling eyes. Jimmy did his best to stare right back.

"I'm a gentleman. I always offer the lady a taste."

"She needs to sample her own coke?"

"Not sampling, indulging. And there's always some lost in the field test."

"Think a jury will buy that? Think I buy that?"

"You want me to piss in a cup?"

Becker pretended to think about that, then leaned forward, lowering his voice. "No. That's what I most definitely do not want you to do. Look, I'll stand up for you, but it's time you cleaned house. You need some time, we'll work it out. There's a program, six weeks, over in Bullhead City, you can use an assumed name. It's the best deal you're gonna get. In the meantime, wrap this up. You've got your case, close it out."

Jimmy felt a surge of bile boiling in his stomach—at the thought of rehab, sure, the shame of it, the tedium, but not just that. "Like when?"

"Like now." Becker's whole face said: Look at yourself. "Why wait?"

Jimmy pictured Sam in her sundress, face raised to the light, hand in her hair. Moisture pooling in the hollow of her throat. Lipstick glistening in the heat.

He said, "There's a kid involved."

Becker stood up behind his desk. They were done. "Get CPS involved, that's what they're there for. Make the calls, do the paperwork, get it over with."

"FOR CHRISSAKE, don't over-think it. Sounds like the last nice guy in Vegas."

It was Mandy talking, Sam's old best friend at the Roundup. She'd stopped by on her way to work, a gram for the shift, and now was lingering, shoes off, stocking feet on the coffee table, toes jigging in their sheer cocoon. They were watching Natalie play, noticing how her focus lasered from her ball to her bear, back to the ball, moving on to her always mysterious foot, then a housefly buzzing at the sliding glass door.

"Dating the clientele," Sam said, "is such a chump move."

"Rules have exceptions. Otherwise, they wouldn't be rules."

Natalie hefted herself onto her feet, staggered to the sliding glass door, reached for the fly—awestruck, gentle.

"He's got a bit of a problem." Sam tapped the side of her nose.

"You can clean him up. Woman's work."

"I don't need that kind of project."

"If you don't mind my asking, how long's it been since you got laid?"

Admittedly, sometimes when Jimmy was there, Sam felt the old urge uncoiling inside her, slithering around. "To be honest, I do mind you asking."

They weren't close anymore, just one of those things. To

hide her disappointment, Mandy softly clapped her hands at Natalie. "Hey sweetheart, come on over. Sit with Auntie Man a little while." The little girl ignored her, still enchanted by the fly. It careened about the room—ceiling, lamp shade, end table—then whirled back to the sliding glass door, a glossy green speck in a flaring pool of sunlight.

"She doesn't like me."

"She can be persnickety." Sam glanced at the clock. "Don't take it personally."

"You think if you let this guy know you were interested, he'd respond?"

Sam felt another headache coming on. Each one seemed worse than the last now. "It's not an issue."

"You're the one playing hard to get, not him."

Jimmy's last visit, Sam had almost thrown herself across his lap, wanting to feel his arms around her. Just that. But that was everything, could be everything. "I've given him a few openings. Nothing obvious, but since when do you need to be obvious with men?"

Mandy crossed her arms across her midriff, as though suddenly chilled. "Maybe he's queer."

ONCE MANDY WAS GONE, Sam tucked Natalie in for the midday nap with her blue plush piglet, brushing the hair from the little girl's face to plant a kiss on her brow. Leaving the bedroom door slightly ajar—Natalie would never drop off otherwise—Sam fled to her own room and took a Demerol. The pain was flashing through her sinuses now, even pulsing into her spine. Noticing the time, she changed into a cinched sleeveless dress, freshened her lipstick, her eyeliner. Jimmy had said he'd stop by, and she still couldn't quite decide whether to push the ball into his end of the court or abide by her own better instincts and let it go. Running a mental inventory of his pros and cons, she admitted he was a joy to look at, had a soldier's good manners, adored Natalie. He was also a flaming cokehead, with the predictable sidekick, a blind thirst. Those things trended downward in her experience, not a ride she wanted to share. Loneliness is the price you pay for keeping things uncomplicated, she thought, pressing a tissue between her lips.

She heard a shuffle of steps on the walkway out front, but instead of ringing the bell, whoever it was pounded at the door. A voice she didn't recognize called out her name, then: "Police! Open the door." To her shame, she froze. Out of the corner of her eye she saw three men cluster on the patio—shirtsleeves, sunglasses, protective vests—and her mouth turned to dust. The front door crashed in, brutal shouts of "On the floor!" and shortly she was facedown, being handcuffed, feeling guilty and terrified and stupid and numb while cops thrashed everywhere, asserting claim to every room.

When they pulled her to her feet, it was Jimmy standing there, wearing a vest like the others, his police card hanging by a thong around his neck. The Demerol not having yet kicked in, her head crackled and throbbed with a new burst of pain, and she feared she might hurl right there on the floor.

"Tell us where everything is, and we won't take the place apart," he said, regarding her with a look of such contemptuous loathing she actually thought he might spit in her face. And I deserve it, she told herself, how stupid I've been, at the same time thinking: Now who's the creature? She could smell the scotch on his breath, masked with spearmint. So that's what it was, she thought, all that time, the drink, the coke. Mr. Sensitive drowning his guilt. Or was even his guilt phony?

She said, "What about Natalie?" In her room, the little girl was mewling, confused, scared.

Jimmy glanced off toward the sound, eyes dull as lead. "She's a ward of the court now. They'll farm her out, foster home—"

Sam felt the room close in, a sickly shade of white. "Why are you doing this?"

Almost imperceptibly, he stiffened. A weak smile. "I'm doing this?"

"Why are you being such a prick about it?"

He leaned in. His eyes were electric. "You're a mother."

You miserable hypocrite, she thought, trying to muster some disgust of her own, but instead her knees turned liquid. He caught her before she fell, duck-walked her toward the sofa, let her drop—at which point a woman with short sandy hair came out of Natalie's bedroom, carrying the little girl. Her eyes were puffy with sleep but she was squirming, head swiveling this way and that. She began to cry. Sam shook off her daze, turned to hide the handcuffs, calling out, "Just do what the lady says, baby. I'll come get you as soon as I can," but the girl started shrieking, kicking—and then was gone.

"Get a good look?" Jimmy said. "Because that's the last you'll see of her."

He was performing for the other cops, the coward. "You can't do that."

"No? Consider it done."

Sam struggled to her feet. "You can't ... No ... "

He nudged her back down. She tried to kick him but he pushed her legs aside. Crouching down, he locked them against his body with one arm, his free hand gripping her chin. Voice lowered, eyes fixed on hers—and, finally, she thought she saw something hovering behind the savage bloodshot blue, something other than the arrogance and hate, something haunted, like pity, even love—he whispered, "Listen to me, Sam. I want to help you. But you've gotta help me. Understand? Give me a name. It's that simple. A name and we work this out. I'll do everything I can, that's a promise, for you, for Natalie—everything. But you've gotta hold up your end. Otherwise ..."

He let his voice trail away into the nothingness he was offering. For Sam knew where this led, she remembered the words exactly: *I have men who take care of certain matters ... The time will have passed for you to say or do anything to help yourself ...*

And there it was: her daughter or her life, she couldn't save both. Maybe not today or tomorrow but someday soon, Claudia's threat would materialize, assuming a face and form but no name—the police would promise protection, but the desert was littered with their failures—and Sam would realize this is it, that pitiless point in time when she would finally know: Which was she? One of those who tried to kick and claw and scream her way out, even though it was hopeless. Or one of those who, seeing there was no escape, calmly said, I'm ready. I've been ready for a long, long while.

The Axiom
of Choice

AS I SAT HERE WAITING, wondering how to explain things, I caught myself remembering something often said about set theory. I teach mathematics at the college, I'm sure you know that already. It's sometimes described—set theory, I mean, excuse me—it's oftentimes described as a field in which nothing is self-evident: True statements are often paradoxical and plausible ones are false. I can imagine you describing your own line of work much the same way. If not, by the time I'm finished here, I suspect you will.

I see by your ring you're married. Perhaps you'll agree with me that marriage, like life itself, is never quite what one expects.

I've even heard it said that, sooner or later, one's wife becomes a sister or an enemy. I'm sure for a great many men that's true. I'd put it differently. Again, if I can borrow a phrase from my area of expertise, I suppose I might say of Veronica's essential nature—her soul for lack of a better term—what Descartes said of infinity: It's something I could recognize but not comprehend.

Now, I can imagine you thinking, given what you saw in our bedroom, that such a statement reveals a profound bitterness, even hatred. I assure you that's not the case. But there's no getting inside another person, no rummaging around inside a wife's or a lover's psyche the way you might dig through a drawer. The gulf between me and my wife, her and Aydin—that's the name of the young man whose body you found beside my wife's: Aydin Donnelly, he was my student—the gulf between any two people may feel negligible at times, intimacy being the intoxicant it is, but the chasm remains unbridgeable. It has nothing to do with facts—my God, who has a greater accumulation of *facts* than a married couple? No, I'm not speaking out of bitterness. On the contrary, I feel humbled by this observation. What I mean to say is this: If you simply bother to reflect on the matter seriously, or just open your eyes, absolutely everything, even oneself—and especially one's wife—remains mysterious.

Veronica and I met at university—which school isn't important, one of those giant Midwestern diploma mills attended by middle-class *untermenschen* on the cusp of discovering their utter ordinariness. I was finishing my doctoral studies in math, she was pursuing music.

Veronica's instrument was the viola. There's a joke about violists, perhaps you know it. *What is the difference between a coffin and a viola? With a coffin, the corpse is on the inside.* Tasteless, I know, considering the circumstances. What I mean is that

Veronica, for most of her life, lacked the expressiveness, the passion, to be anything but merely functional as a performer. She had an excellent memory and commendable dexterity, she fooled a great many people. But there was a wooden, colorless quality to her playing that no amount of practice could transform. She realized early on that she would be a teacher, like me—and yes, when I spoke of utter ordinariness, you didn't think I was excluding myself, did you?

We met the way most graduate students do—in the library. I wonder how many campus marriages find their beginnings in the stacks. Such a strangely erotic locale—the order, the stillness, it cries out for something heated and spontaneous, something messy. But we did not desecrate the library. Not Veronica's style.

By that point she was already recognizing her limitations. The company of other music majors only hammered that home, so she steered clear of the music building, holidayed over to the main library to study and one day by chance took up position across the table from me. Luck is the heart of romance, they say, not fate. I cannot dispute that.

I was torturing myself in preparation for my orals. Almost every great mind in mathematics did his most creative work by the age of eighteen. I was twenty-five at that point—a confirmed mediocrity, struggling with all my might not to become a joke. Veronica plopped herself down not three feet away, spread out her sheet music for compositional analysis—it was Bach, of course. Musicians uncertain of their talent always gravitate toward the Baroque: so dense, so artificial. Music to hide behind.

I know I sound callous but that's not at all my intent. The state in which you found Veronica is hideous. Perhaps you took the time to look at some of the pictures around the house. If so, you saw that she was quite lovely in her way, bigger than is considered fashionable, I suppose, but when has fashion ever understood women? I found her softness beguiling. I'm hardly svelte, obviously, but it's different with men.

Such a shy, defenseless smile—that's what I noticed when I glanced up that first time and saw her across the table. Of course, like everyone else in that library she was frightened, overwhelmed, miserable with doubt, but she looked at me so sweetly. I wasn't one to believe love could solve my life but I was overdue for a little kindness.

We popped out for coffee, the ritual chat, feeling each other out, where we came from, where we hoped to go. The kindness, I learned, was genuine. Soon enough, we were inseparable. It's hard to describe to people who've never known it, the pressure, the grinding isolation of graduate school. A great many campus marriages are formed from the simple need for companionship and commiseration. Ours was. We were lonely, we tended not to get on each other's nerves, we respected each other's privacy. The next thing we knew, five years had gone by. I received my position here at the college, she found herself a chair in the local chamber orchestra.

Eventually, as all couples do, we had our problems. Veronica was too self-conscious to genuinely enjoy sex—that may seem overly personal, what my students refer to as Too Much Information, but I'd be surprised if you hadn't been waiting for me to bring it up. What I mean is, abandon was not a quality she possessed or aspired to possess—that too showed in her playing. I won't psychoanalyze her for you, drag out all the family trash, but shame factored heavily in her upbringing. She could pet and kiss and cuddle, I never felt a lack of affection, but—excuse me, again, if this sounds coarse—good old-fashioned fucking was simply too intrusive.

To her credit she didn't find my appetites perverse or unwholesome. She did not love me less because of what I wanted. So—a sister or an enemy. I suppose one could say Veronica became my sister, though that's both too cynical and too superficial a way to put it. It was decided I would have my affairs, as long as they remained dalliances and not devotions. She would keep her home, which she suffered over as only a woman can. The marriage would remain intact.

You may think me a monster at this point. But reflect on what I just said: We reached an understanding—how many couples fail or refuse to do that? Part of that understanding was that I would stay. I did. Right up until the end.

You're probably asking yourself: How did this man ever get anyone but his wife to so much as look at him? Trust me, I'm not unaware of my homeliness. I used to wear a beard as a sort of disguise, it gave me a bearish, rakehell appeal, or so I liked to think. But I'm not blind to what an unlikely Lothario I make.

I've even talked about it with some of the woman I've been with, a few of whom were by any objective standard completely out of my league. And I've heard this response often enough now to consider it more than likely to be true: A great many men simply don't like sex. They either find it a messy obligation involving smells and feelings they abhor, or a kind of athletic event at which their prowess must never be questioned. Well, I don't share such inhibitions, and I'm not shy about my pleasures. It's amazing how appealing that can be to a woman. Especially a woman who, like me, is cheating on her spouse.

Now, I can imagine what you're thinking. Anyone who walks away from the scene you discovered in my house, then talks about his sex life, his lack of inhibition, his pleasures—not to mention set theory and Descartes, for God's sake—you have to wonder: Is he demented? Is he a sociopath? Or, on a far more rudimentary level: Is he lying?

I assure you, I am not deranged, nor do I lack a conscience. As for lying—well, that's always an interesting question, isn't it? I'm sure you're aware of the Liar's Paradox. Consider the statement, "I am lying." If the statement is true, it means I'm not lying when I say I'm lying, which is nonsense. Contrarily, if the statement is false, it means I'm lying when I say I'm lying and thus I'm telling the truth. Again, ridiculous. I can only imagine every cop in the world knows that one, not to mention the average nine-year-old.

You may not know this, but paradoxes like that were the bane of mathematics at the turn of the last century. Damn near brought the whole field to a screaming halt. And paradoxes—or antinomies, as they're now called—are always the sort of thing that most fascinate my students, which brings us at last to Aydin.

The name's Turkish. Curiously enough, it means "enlightened." I told you his surname: Donnelly. A particularly intriguing American mutt—workaholic father of famine Irish stock, Turkish-German scold for a mother. All that unruly black hair, those Levantine eyes, the bucket-shaped head and nail-driver hands. Even his slump was oddly beguiling—he looked burdened.

Aydin attended my course on the history of mathematics—an easy "A" for those in the humanities needing a science credit. I don't fool myself regarding my function on campus. It's a small liberal arts college of no particular reputation, a dumping ground basically for those with little promise beyond money. My job is to help them toward a degree so they don't further embarrass their families. A little calculus, maybe an intro to stat, remedial trig for most of them—all topped off with a course on the *history* of mathematics, the *philosophy* of science. It's about as much rigor as the poor darlings can stand.

Aydin stood out to the extent he actually made an effort to pay attention. Believe me, that's enough to endear a student to a teacher these days. I looked forward to his visits to my office. His conversation, if not exactly profound, at least displayed some fire.

He developed a fascination with what is known as the Axiom of Choice—I assure you this is relevant. It's a fundamental principle that states we can create a new set by choosing one item from each of an infinite number of other sets. There, simple to state, but the idea is implicitly fantastical: Who would do the choosing? When would he finish? Never, of course, by definition the task is infinite. The physical universe would come to an end before the selection process was complete.

But by assuming that the task can be accomplished, by acting as though we can step outside time and treat infinities like common objects, we find ourselves capable of constructing the lion's share of modern mathematics. Deny ourselves this trick, we close the door to much of what we have accomplished for the past century—and these achievements are astonishing, not just in abstract mathematics but the applied sciences. All those little geniuses out on the quad, listening to their iPods or thumbing away on their iPhones—not even gizmos of that order would be possible without the Axiom of Choice, let alone advances in advanced circuitry and theoretical physics. It's one of the great ironies of modernity. By turning a blind eye to an intellectual sleight of hand, we have created some of the greatest tools for understanding the physical world in human history.

All of this fascinated Aydin, but he was inclined to fuzzy thinking—one of those easily distracted, poetic souls who get snarled in a confusion and think they've beheld the profound.

For him the Axiom of Choice got all mixed up with other things, like the notion that real world success necessarily results from self-delusion. That appealed to him in a fundamental way, something to do with his father I think. The man's a securities lawyer in Chicago, very connected, impressively rich. To Aydin, he was a pompous phony. My point, though, is that the young man obsessed over the ways we fool ourselves, and so the Axiom of Choice became a kind of a symbol for our inescapable self-deceit. We trick ourselves into believing in freedom, for example, when in truth everything's preordained. We're hormonal robots, he said, prisoners of biology. All of which is just warmed-over Platonism. And as Plato himself so deftly pointed out, the inescapable implication is that we're all just shadows.

But Aydin took it a step further. If choice is an illusion, then there's also no responsibility. If you had him here in this chair, not me, that's what he'd tell you. Even murder is nothing more than the turning of a page in some inscrutable book. And there's the greatest paradox of all, he'd say: We convince ourselves we're free in order to escape the terror of realizing it doesn't matter. The game's been over from the start.

This sort of thinking is very common among the young. They worry themselves sick about authenticity because they sense themselves to be, at root, fundamentally inauthentic. For Christ's sake, they haven't lived yet, what is there to be authentic about? I try to tell them that. In particular, I tried to tell Aydin. But he was obsessively earnest the way only a twenty-year-old of middling intelligence can be, which is why he appealed so much to Veronica.

Veronica was devoted to strays. If you were lost, she found you. And Aydin was desperately, irretrievably lost. You could see from the scars on his wrists he'd made a hash of at least one suicide attempt. That too seems to be required for modern adolescence, like computers and tattoos. But it only stirred Veronica's pity.

They met when she stopped by my office late one day, picking me up for some dinner engagement with the director of the chamber orchestra—God, there's something I won't miss. She paid poor Aydin little mind, being preoccupied, but there was no mistaking *his* reaction. He stared at her as though she were literally incandescent.

Here again, you may think me a monster, but I found Aydin's infatuation the perfect solution to a problem. He could be the pet Veronica craved, a way to nourish her insatiable need to be *involved*. God knows Aydin was in desperate want of a woman's *involvement*. Maybe I felt guilty—I was having a particularly heated liaison at the time, a woman in Veronica's string section no less.

How did I hatch my plan? I invited Aydin over to dinner—there, simple, like sin itself. And all I had to do was wait for him to reach for something, expose those tortured wrists—Veronica's eyes popped like flashbulbs. After we cleared plates and put on the kettle for tea I feigned a need for some air to give them the necessary privacy. I knew Aydin would take care of the rest. He'd say it was predetermined.

You'll find this absurd but I honestly did not foresee their becoming sexual. Oh, I didn't doubt they might come to exchange some tenderness, and I could well imagine poor sad Aydin planting his face between Veronica's ample tits to weep. But sex? As I said, I recognized my wife but did not comprehend her. The shame surrounding her body, her uneasiness with anything untidy—well, apparently that had far more to do with me specifically than either of us realized.

But that wasn't all I didn't see coming. Veronica lost weight. Her playing improved dramatically—she gave a solo recital of the Sonata Pastorale and seemed a different person during the performance. She blossomed, became the woman she'd secretly wanted to be all along. And she had Aydin, not me, to thank for that. She calmed him down. He made her feel needed.

Now, if I were you, I'd hear all this and be thinking: Here's a man who thought he had life figured out, an understanding wife, a slice on the side—do people still say it that way?—every need gratified. Then he discovers that in fact he had it all wrong. Not just that, but his wife's aversion to good old-fashioned fucking, as he put it, was really just revulsion for him. How humiliating. Must've royally pissed him off.

I wouldn't fault you for jumping to such a conclusion. But you'd be wrong. I loved my wife. I was happy for her. I was pleased she'd solved the riddle of her sexual indifference, even if it was less than flattering to me. As I said, I knew how to find gratification elsewhere. We should all be happy, the world being what it is.

And no, this isn't where my wife stopped being a sister and began life as my enemy. That would be ironic, yes, but what actually occurred was even more ridiculous: I lost all interest in other women. As a kind of penance, a way to own my faithlessness, I shaved off my beard. All of which, of course, was secretly a way to prepare myself for returning to Veronica's affections. Like some character in a farce I began to long for her in a way I never knew I could. But she would not entertain my interests there—who could blame her? Even so, I wanted to be worthy of her when her liaison with Aydin finally ran its course. And yes, I believed that was inevitable. Veronica and I would rediscover each other. I knew that as certainly as I knew anything. What I didn't anticipate was how it would occur, but I'm getting ahead of myself.

We actually managed to live agreeably, the three of us, for nearly a year. I grew into my newfound humility, even as Aydin became prone to fits of indignation—he had rights, don't you know. Talk about smug. Thank God Veronica put him straight on such nonsense. This is how it is, she said, you can behave or be alone. After a day or two of miserable fuming he'd come around. But honestly, episodes like that were quite rare. He wasn't a bad young man. He was just so damn sentimental.

Then Veronica began having these odd pains in her joints. She wondered if it weren't some kind of arthritis, every musician's nightmare. Soon her breathing became labored. The nurse at our doctor's office referred her for a sonogram. The results indicated she had what was euphemistically described as a "complex mass." It turned out to be Stage IV clear-cell epithelial ovarian cancer. A death sentence.

If you doubt my love for my wife, ask the doctors and nurses at the cancer clinic what sort of husband I was once Veronica fell sick. I'm not bragging—I can think of nothing more hideous than taking pride in being a commendable Joe when one's wife is dying—but I need to make sure you don't misunderstand the true nature of what happened. That's very important to me. And my behavior stood in stark contrast to Aydin's. Just when he could have done us all a favor and grown up, he reverted to the most grotesque childishness. Suddenly only he understood what Veronica needed. I was complicating her relationship with the nurses at the clinic. I was confusing her, confusing the doctors, all out of some perverse narcissism. I've no doubt he blamed the cancer itself on me, my neglect of her sexually all those years.

Meanwhile, things at home grew increasingly hard. Veronica's hair began falling out with the chemo and she decided to
have it all shaved off. That, combined with the dark patches
under her eyes, the grayish tint of her skin—I removed as many
mirrors as I could. Add to that the mental confusion, the lack of
balance, the nausea, the pain—such a miserable, pitiless, degrad-
ing way to die. As for music, she wanted nothing to do with it,
threw a fit if the radio was on. It reminded her of everything that
would never be.

Don't get me wrong, there were also days when Veronica
was incredibly heroic. She could be so outgoing, especially to
other patients at the clinic. But yes, she could also be petty and
bitter and scared. She was human, for Christ's sake.

Meanwhile, Aydin seemed to think the tragedy was his. I
couldn't keep him away from the house. Trying to explain that
she needed rest only degenerated into screaming matches, so I
invariably relented. Veronica, true to her nature, couldn't refuse
him. She was the one dying but he was the one who needed care.
He'd finally become authentic.

I will admit, yes, that infuriated me. But what came next
cannot be laid solely at the door of my rage.

Last night, about nine or so, Veronica started screaming
suddenly from the bedroom. She'd been asleep and a nightmare woke her—she dreamed she was drowning from the fluid
building up in her lungs. She was terrified: Don't let me die like
that, she begged. I called the on-duty nurse, asked her to talk
Veronica down, explain to her what was happening. The nurse
told her that no, she wouldn't drown, most likely she'd die as her
organs shut down one by one. It wasn't a painful way to go, she
said. Veronica snapped back: And how could you possibly know
that? By this point, after all the chirpy prognoses followed by

one round of bad news after the next, she was convinced absolutely everyone was lying.

She asked me to get my gun and shoot her. She couldn't take it anymore, she wanted to put an end to it all, stop dragging it out: Kill me, she said. Please. If you love me, you'll do that for me.

I told her I couldn't. We needed to see the current chemotherapy regimen through to the end to learn if there was any progress. If not, there were other regimens and even clinical trials, experimental treatments. It was far too soon to give up, I said. But we both knew I was being dishonest. Worse, selfish. The thing neither of us dared to say? She was going to die and I was not. She'd run out of luck. If I did as she asked, killed her, I'd be surrendering my luck as well. Perhaps she needed to know I understood what she was going through, what it felt like. Perhaps she wanted vengeance on the thousands of humiliations I'd inflicted on her during our marriage. Perhaps both. Regardless, I saw the demand as unfair. I felt sorry for her. But I refused to give up the rest of my life for her.

What a miserable night. Sleep was out of the question—we talked, we argued, we wept. She remained afraid and ready to die. I remained unwilling to oblige her. All the while, we both danced around the real issue lying there between us. But something else happened too. I've already said I recognized Veronica but did not comprehend her—and once her connection with Aydin took hold I didn't entirely recognize her either. Well, that night, as I faced her hour after hour, trying to reason with her, trying not to get swallowed up by the despair that was dragging her under, my lack of recognition became complete. The chafing voice, the vacant eyes. The hollowed-out ruin her face had become. I no longer saw her there. I saw someone else. I saw myself.

Come morning, Aydin appeared. The night had taken its toll, I'm sure it showed. He asked what was wrong and I simply lacked the wherewithal to make up a lie. He was horrified— not at Veronica's wanting to die but my refusal to do what she wanted. He called me a weakling, a coward. How could I let her continue to suffer? Of course, the real question was: How could I continue to let *him* suffer? He couldn't bear the sight of her misery anymore. He wanted it over with. Christ, who didn't?

I wouldn't let him in. He flew into a rage right there on the porch—neighbors peeked out past their curtains at us—but this time I refused to bend. He wasn't used to being denied. Incensed, he said that before she'd fallen ill, Veronica confessed that she intended to leave me, divorce me, rid herself of me once and for all. She'd come to despise me, then he rattled off all the things she loathed about me, how cold, how resentful, how selfish, how predictable I am. How ugly in every conceivable way. To have this shouted in my face, by a boy, after the night I'd just spent—especially while harboring the ridiculous illusion that, had Victoria's luck been different, she would have returned to me—I will admit, I did not respond wisely. I'm sure you know this, sure the neighbors told you. I shouted right back that, if he didn't leave, I'd kill him.

He shambled off, seething. An hour or so later I had to step out. Veronica was short of Fentanyl patches, I needed to run to the pharmacy. It's hard to describe the level of distraction I've been operating under, one minute panicked into focus, the next I'm standing somewhere, at the sink or in a parking lot, completely oblivious to how much time has passed. And today, as I wandered around the drugstore, God only knows how long, I got lost in my own self-pity, wondering how I could have been such a fool not to grasp Veronica's true feelings. I miss things,

is what I mean to say, things I should have noticed. Like the
fact that, when I drove away from the house, Aydin was nearby,
watching me leave, probably hiding in the park down the block.

When I got back home from the pharmacy I could feel it,
the stillness. I called out. The house swallowed up the sound.

Perhaps Veronica let him in, perhaps I forgot to lock the
door, like I said I've been strangely abstracted of late. I climbed
the stairs, went to the bedroom, found them. I guess it was his
turn to calm her down, her turn to make him feel needed.

She must have told him where I kept my gun—I didn't
see any signs he went scavenging for it himself. Of course, he
botched it, like he had before, only now he'd included Veronica.
He'd fired one round into her skull, but couldn't bother to see if
she was actually dead before turning the gun on himself. That
would have sullied the drama. He was very sentimental, like I
said, yes, which is just another way of saying he was incompetent.
But what's the point of competence if you're never responsible?

I'm sorry. I sound angry. Bitter, yes. I suppose I am. But not
at Aydin. Not at Veronica. Not anymore.

I stood there wondering: What to do? I could leave, pretend
I'd never come home, let a few hours pass so they could lie there
like that until they finally got what they'd wanted—would that
be denying them anything? Or I could call 911, have the paramedics rush over, fuss over them, dash them off to emergency,
maybe even save them. For what—so Veronica could suffer even
worse than before, only to die in a few weeks regardless? And
Aydin—say he lived, what would he wake up to? Imagine it.
Imagine discovering yourself in a hospital bed, instead of hell
where you belonged. I understood that. I understood because I
realized that's how I'd spent every day of my life, finding myself
unjustifiably alive, furtively killing everything around me.

I'm a coward, yes. They were right: I'm selfish and shallow and vain and weak. And yet oddly enough—here's one more paradox for you—it was Aydin, the one who believed in fate, the one who believed that nothing changes, we are who we are, for better, for worse, forever: He was the one who gave me one last chance. The chance to redefine myself. He'd done what I couldn't bring myself to do—he failed at it, but why punish him for that? Why punish either of them? I tugged the gun from his hand, then took a moment. I had to collect myself, wait until it wasn't revenge or disgust or rage in my heart. Maybe it was just one more trick of the mind, the self-delusion that makes the rest possible, but I told myself: Remember, you know what it means to be overdue for a little kindness.

Stray

CHRISTMAS PATRONS THRONGED the bank. Outside, rain fell, third day running.

All these bodies should warm things up, Marybeth thought, but no. Still, there were festive touches about—harp and dulcimer carols piping softly in the background, twirled bunting draping the walls, ribboned wreaths the size of tires. She caught a hint of pine, drifted into memory. Sacrament of childhood, she thought, this time of year.

She stood in the teller queue, trembling. Be calm, she told herself. Calm as a mutt by a midday fire—Jamie's turn of phrase. He had so many expressions, most of a darker sort: vivid as a cat's ass, face like a bulldog licking piss off a nettle, cold as my dear mother's heart. That bitter turn of mind, so Celtic, but that was why she loved him.

From the very start the attraction lay precisely in what others might call his failures. Success held little appeal for her. Always something brittle about success, something garish, too lucky. She preferred her men wounded but resolved. Solemn determination had greater purchase in her heart than confidence. A man who knew the edge was only a footfall away and who was thinking of how to grab you back from it, protect you, not because he was scared but because he'd made that fall himself once or twice, loved you too much to wish it on you—that was the fella for her.

The queue advanced a step, everyone trudged forward, squeaky boots, soggy shoes. Not much in the way of merry in the faces, she thought, eyeing the others in line. Despite herself, she glanced over her shoulder at the guard near the door. He was hardly more than a boy, his uniform draped on his bone-thin body like a hand-me-down on a rack—a Latino, face dotted with acne, hair gelled into a black shiny wave frozen in time, thumbs tucked in his belt—no gun, just pepper spray. Good, she supposed, feeling a bit less afraid.

Sensing her gaze, perhaps, he turned toward her and met her eyes. Unable to help herself, she smiled. He returned a smile of his own, self-effacing and slack, then reconsidered, averting his face toward the door, but in that instant she detected not one of those sullen, antsy, me-first young men she so despised and feared. Instead she caught a little of the lonely, the lost.

What is it with me, she thought, and strays?

She looked down at the purse she'd brought, one of those shapeless sack-like vinyl things you could get so cheap along Market Street, the Salvation Army bells ringing all around you as you browsed the vendor racks and stalls. Would it be big enough, she wondered, was it too big? She nudged it with her foot along the floor as the line inched ahead.

She'd met Jamie two Januarys past, at the Horn & Whistle, her neighborhood pub, the holidays well behind them, just the bleak cold wind and metal-gray sky, the empty promise of a new year. But then there he was, and promise beckoned.

He was a charmer, yes, the sandy-colored hair, the milky Irish skin and rust-brown freckles, the chesty laugh and the endless string of slightly cruel jokes. A pint of stout, that's what he ordered for her, like a black liquor soup, topped with creamy foam. She nursed it as they got acquainted, she a teacher at city college, remedial composition—a tragedy, how poorly most young people read and wrote these days—and he was in sales, something involving computers, she never did grasp it completely.

Ireland was the new promised land for the digerati then, and he'd worked in Dublin for a while, earned his degrees and certificates, then come over with a cousin, acquired one of those visas Silicon Valley was sponsoring right and left a decade back. He soon tired of the whole mega-corporate slog, went off with a few cohorts to start their own venture, a freelance affair, striking that right balance, enough coin on hand to keep the wolves at bay, enough freedom in his heart to feel like a man. There were setbacks, sure, and he told her about them and they broke her heart. He knew what it meant to fail, then pick himself up, have a pint, share a laugh, get on with it. Leave self-pity to the Russians and Mexicans, he said. Dreams get dashed so new dreams can take their place. They drank to dreams. And she knew in the pit of her heart they would marry.

A mere four weeks later, they did. Valentine's Day. The courthouse, two strangers for witnesses.

She suddenly found herself at the head of the queue, and a queasy lightheadedness came over her. She bit back the nausea, dabbed at her face with the back of her wool glove.

The house was Jamie's idea. No better investment than property, he'd said, San Francisco property in particular. What about the recession, she'd said, and he'd answered that's why the timing's perfect. Buy low, sell dear. There's still no way we can manage it, she'd told him, but he'd taken rein of the finances— a husband's mortal obligation, his words—and he knew a man who knew a man and said trust me and how could she not? And then there they were, a two-bedroom bungalow bordering Noe Valley, a fixer-upper for sure, but home.

She left her job with its benefits to manage the most essential repairs, emptied her savings to pay for them—the kitchen and bath had to be gutted, rebuilt from the floor joists up, so much dry rot, and she blamed the ache in her joints on all the physical labor, pitching in with the workers—while Jamie, suit and tie and freshly shined shoes, went out each day to slay the beast. Solemn determination. Protecting her.

It took until Thanksgiving for him to confess the truth. There was no job, hadn't been for over a year. He just rode the bus from one end of the city to the other, or sometimes he'd get on the train, ride down to San Jose or out to Walnut Creek, the suburban outposts, all those majestic hills and bustling malls, all the traffic and the nouveau riche. The mortgage lender, in truth a den of crooks Marybeth could hardly believe existed, filed their notices, moved to foreclose and evict—a scam from the start, and she wondered if Jamie had been duped or complicit. Regardless, two days after the last papers were served, she had her consult, learned her joint aches were not arthritis but something much worse.

The teller near the end came free and beckoned Marybeth forward. She reached down, snatched up the giant floppy purse, trundled over. The teller said something festive in greeting but

49

Marybeth barely heard, it was like she was underwater, rustling around in the bag for the envelope and remembering what Jamie had said the day he'd left: You deserve someone better, I can only drag you down, I'm nothing, a wretch, a failure. I know, she'd thought, I'm a lover of failures, it's my curse, wanting to tell him—I have cancer, it's in my bone marrow—but the words wouldn't come.

Finally, she felt it, the card, brought it out and, hand shaking as though from palsy, slipped it across the counter to the teller. A plump girl, heavy-lidded eyes, flat nose, chestnut hair. She lifted the flap on the envelope, withdrew the Christmas card, inside of which Marybeth had written: *I have a gun. Do not trigger the alarm or make a sound. Give me all the money in your cashier tray or I will shoot, one by one, the customers standing in line behind me.*

Her heart bucked inside her chest as she hefted the huge bag onto the counter for the teller to fill. A note job, they called it—in truth there was no gun, and she hoped she'd get consideration for that when they prosecuted her. Glancing about to see who was staring—no one, it turned out, not yet—she listened to the fluttery thump of the banded stacks of bills as the teller stuffed them inside the purse. Then a sudden flare of pain shot through her, ripping through her bones like black fire. No, she thought, not now, and she steadied herself, grabbed the purse, then glanced at the teller whose eyes were scared and resentful.

"I'm sorry," Marybeth whispered as she turned away, shouldering the purse, surprised at its toppling weight, then staggered toward the young Latino guard. A few of the other patrons finally seemed aware of what had happened, there were whispers and stares but Marybeth paid no heed. Her eyes remained fixed on the guard with his stiff wavelike hair, his expression first puzzled then alarmed as she plodded closer.

"I've just stolen this." Grimacing from the pain, she dropped the purse at his feet. They both stared at it. "You need to arrest me, or call the police, if that's how it's done."

Last week, in a magazine that someone had left behind in the bus shelter, she'd read that women could get chemotherapy in prison. And a bank robbery meant federal custody, better care. By no means good care, she thought, but a small hope is still hope, almost collapsing as the young guard glanced down into the bag, saw the money, then looked back at her, panic in his eyes. So young, she thought. Christmas is for the young.

"I'm not crazy." Her voice was clenched. "Sick, yes, you can probably tell. But not mad."

He still seemed paralyzed. Fearing she might faint before he understood, she took his hand, clutched it tight. So helpless, she thought, a stray. "Please," she said softly. "Help me."

It Can Happen

PILGRIM WATCHED AS, just outside his bedroom door, Lorene handed Robert fifty dollars and told him she wanted to visit personal with her ex-husband for a spell. Robert was Pilgrim's nurse. He'd been a wrestler in college—you had to be strong to heft a paralyzed man in and out of bed—and worked sometimes now as a bouncer on his off-hours.

Robert glanced back toward the bedroom for approval and Pilgrim gave his nod. The big man pocketed the money, donned his hat and walked out the door in his whites, not bothering with his coat despite the cold.

Pilgrim liked that about Robert—his strength, his vigor, his indifference to life's little bothers. Maybe 'liked' wasn't quite the word. Envied.

He lay back in bed and waited for Lorene to rejoin him.

His room was the largest in the cramped, dreary house and bare except for the twenty thousand dollar wheel chair gathering dust in the corner, the large-screen TV he was so very tired of watching, an armchair for visitors with a single lamp beside it and the centerpiece—the mechanical bed, a hospital model, tilted up so he didn't just lie flat all day.

Lorene took up position bedside and crossed her arms. She was a pretty, short, ample, strong woman. "Don't make me go off on you."

Pilgrim tilted his head to see her, eyes glazed. Every ten minutes or so, someone needed to wipe the fluid away. It was a new problem, the tear ducts. Three years now since the accident, reduced to deadweight from the neck down, followed by organs failing, musty skin, powdery hair, his body in a slow but inexorable race with his mind to the grave. He was forty-three years old.

In a scratchy whisper, he said, "I got my eyes and ears out there."

"Corella?" Their daughter. Corella the Giver, Lorene called her, not kindly.

"You been buying things," he said.

"Furniture a crime now?"

"Things you can't afford, not by the wildest stretch—"

"Ain't your business, Pilgrim. My home, we're talkin' about." She pressed her finger against her breastbone. "Mine."

Lorene lived in a renovated Queen Anne Victorian in the Excelsior District of San Francisco, hardly an exclusive area but grand next to Hunter's Point, where Pilgrim remained, living in the same house he'd lived in on a warehouseman's salary, barely more than a shack.

Pilgrim bought the Excelsior house after his accident, when he came into his money through the legal settlement. He was broadsided by a semi when his brakes failed, a design defect on his lightweight pickup. Lorene stood by him till the money came through then filed for divorce, saying she was still young. She needed a real husband.

Actually, the word she used was "functional."

The divorce was uglier than some, less so than most. The major compromise concerned the Victorian. Her gave her a living estate—it was her residence till she died—but it stayed in his name. He needed that. Lorene would have her lovers, the men would come and go, but he'd still have that cord, connecting them—his love, her guilt. His money, her wants.

He got $12,000 a month from the annuity the truck manufacturer set up. Half of that went to pay Lorene's mortgage, the rest got eaten up by medical bills, twenty-four hour care, medicine, food, utilities. He had no choice but to stay here in this ugly, decrepit, shameful house.

"Know your problem, Pilgrim? You don't get out. Dust off that damn wheelchair and—"

"Catch pneumonia."

"Wrap your damn self up."

"Who is he, Lorene?"

She cocked her head. "Who you mean?"

"The man in the house I pay for."

Lorene put her hands on her hips and rocked a little, back and forth. "No. No, Pilgrim. You and me, we got an understanding. I don't know what Corella's been saying—"

"I know you got men. That's not the point here. You take this one in?"

"You got no say, Pilgrim."

"Even folks at Corella's church know about him. Reverend Williams, he calls himself. Slick as a frog's ass."

"I ain't listening to this."

"All AIDS this and Africa that. But he's running from trouble in Florida somewhere, down around Tampa."

"That's church gossip, Pilgrim. Raymont never even *been* to Tampa."

"Now you spending money hand over fist. That where it's coming from, Lorene? Phony charity, pass the basket? *Raymont?* No. That wouldn't pay the freight, way I hear you re-done that house. What you up to, Lorene? You know I'll find out."

Finally, fear darkened her eyes. He wanted to ask her: What do you expect? Take away a man's body, he still has his heart. Mess with his heart, though, there's nothing left but the hate. And the hate builds.

"Pilgrim, you do me an injustice when you make accusations like that." The words came out with a sad, lukewarm pity. She sighed, slipped off her shoes, motored the bed down till he lay flat then climbed on, straddling him. "This what you after? Then say so." She took a Kleenex from the box on the bed and wiped his puddled eyes, then stroked his face with her fingers, her skin cool against his. She cupped his cheek in her palm and leaned down to kiss him. "Why do you doubt my feelings, Pilgrim?"

"Send him away, Lorene."

"Pilgrim, you gotta let—"

"I'll forgive everything—I don't care what you've done to get the money or how much it is—but you gotta send him away. For good."

Lorene looked deep into Pilgrim's eyes then got down off the bed, slipped her shoes back on and straightened her skirt. "One of these days, Pilgrim—before you die—you're gonna have to accept that I'm not to blame for what happened to you.

And what you want from me, and what I'm able to give, are two entirely different things."

ROBERT RETURNED TO FIND Lorene gone. How long she leave Mr. Baxter alone, he wondered, chastising himself. He checked his watch, barely half an hour since he'd left but that was plenty of time to have an accident. And he ain't gonna blame her, hell no. That witch got the man's paralyzed dick wrapped around her little finger tight as a yo-yo. He's gonna lay blame on me.

That was pretty much the routine between them. Bitch rant scream, beg snivel thank. Return to beginning and start again. Even so, Robert knew he had the makings of a good thing here. He didn't want it jeopardized. Mr. Baxter wasn't long for this life, every day something else went wrong, more and more, faster and faster. The man relied on Robert for all those sad, pathetic, humiliating little tasks no one else would bother with. If Robert played it right, made himself trusted and dependable—the final friend—there could be a little something on the back end worth waiting for.

Everybody working in-home care knew a story. One woman Robert knew personally had tended an old man down in Hillsborough, famously wealthy, and he scribbled on a napkin two days before he passed that she was to get forty thousand dollars from his estate. The family fought it, of course—they were already inheriting millions but that's white people for you—claiming she'd had undue influence over his weakened mind. The point was, though, it can happen. Long as you don't let the family hoodwink you.

Venturing into the bedroom doorway, Robert discovered Pilgrim trembling. His breathing was ragged.

"Mr. Baxter, you all right?"

Edging closer, he saw more tears streaking down the older man's face than leakage could explain. His lip quivered.

"Good Lord, Mr. Baxter? What did that woman do?"

Pilgrim hissed, "Call my lawyer."

MARGUERITE JOHNSTONE HAD GONE to law school to escape Hunter's Point but still had clients in the neighborhood—wills and trusts, conservatorships, probate contests, for those who could afford them. She sat parked at the curb outside Pilgrim's house, waiting a moment behind the wheel, checking to make sure she had the address right.

The place was small and square with peeling paint and a flat, tar-paper roof. In back, a makeshift carport had all but collapsed from dry rot. Weeds had claimed the yard from the grass and grew waist-high. How in God's name, she thought, can a man worth three-quarters of a million dollars live in a dump like this?

It sat at the corner of Fitch and Crisp—Fish & Chips, they used to call it when she lived up the hill on Jerrold—the last residence before the shabby warehouses and noxious body shops rimming the old shipyard. The Redevelopment Agency had big plans for new housing nearby but plans had never been the problem in this part of town. The problem was following through. And if any locals, meaning black folks, actually got a chance to live in what the city finally built up there it would constitute an act of God. Meanwhile, the only construction actually underway was for the light rail and that was lagging, millions over budget, years behind schedule, the muddy trench down Third Street all anyone could point to and say: *There's where the money went.*

The rest of the neighborhood consisted of bland, crumbling little two-story houses painted tacky colors, with iron bars at the windows. At least they looked lived in. There were families here, holding out, waiting for something better to come—where else could they go? And with the new white mayor coming down all the time, making a show of how he cared, people had a right to think maybe now, finally, things would turn around. But come sunset the hoodrats still crawled out, mayor or no mayor, claiming their corners. Making trade. Marguerite made a mental note to wrap things up and get out before dark.

ROBERT LED THE LAWYER through the bedroom door and Pilgrim sized her up. A tall, freckled, coffee-skinned woman with her hair pulled back and tied with a bow, glasses, frumpy suit and flats. Be nicer looking if she made an effort, he thought.

"Nice to meet you," he croaked. "You come well recommended. This here's my daughter."

Corella sat at the end of the bed, dressed in black, down to the socks and shoes, her hair short like a man's. His other daughter, Cynthia, was the pretty one but she wasn't Lorene's child. Cynthia lived with her mother far away, St. Louis the last anybody heard.

Corella would never move away. She was daddy's little princess, homely like him.

Marguerite extended her hand. "Pleasure."

"Obliged," Corella said.

Pilgrim shooed both Robert and his daughter from the room. Robert went quick, Corella less so. Clingy, that was the word he wanted. But bitter. He waited for the door to close.

"I got the feeling," he said, "way your voice sounded over the phone—"

"You were right, there are problems." Marguerite removed a thin stack of papers from her briefcase, copies of documents she'd discovered at the County Recorder. "With the Excelsior property."

She explained what she'd found. Six months earlier, the IRS had filed tax liens for over three hundred thousand dollars in back taxes against a Raymont Williams—who came with a generous assortment of aliases. Soon after that, Lorene, who worked at a local credit union, recorded the first of three powers-of-attorney, forging Pilgrim's signature and getting a notary at the credit union to validate it. Then, acting as Pilgrim's surrogate under the power-of-attorney, she took out a loan for a hundred-twenty thousand dollars, same amount as the oldest of the tax liens, securing it with the Excelsior property.

But no release of lien was ever recorded. Apparently, when Lorene realized how easily she could phony up a loan, she got the fever. The IRS could wait for its money. Two more loans followed for increasingly shameless sums from hard money lenders. The house was now leveraged to the hilt, the total indebtedness over six hundred thousand dollars and that was just principal. Worse, though Lorene had made a token effort to cover her tracks, keep up with the payments, she'd already slipped into default.

"Expects me to come to the rescue," Pilgrim guessed.

"It's that or lose the house to foreclosure," Marguerite said.

"All that happen in just six months?" Pilgrim chided himself for not seeing it sooner. Hadn't even known about this Raymont fool till recent. Why hadn't Corella told him earlier? She went to see her mother from time to time—not often, they didn't get on, but often enough. Daddy's homely, clingy, bitter little princess was playing both sides. But she'd pay. Everyone would pay.

Marguerite said, "You've got a very strong case against the notary, pretty strong against the lenders, though the last two are a step above loan sharks. I don't know what Lorene told them—"

"Woman can charm a stump."

"But they'll want their money. They'll know they can't go against Lorene or this Raymont individual for recovery. And they could say they had a right to rely on the notary and turn on her but her pockets most likely aren't that deep either. So they'll come after you. And my guess is they won't be nice about it."

"How you figure?"

"It'll suit their purposes to stick with Lorene and her story, at least for a while. She'll say she had your full authority to do what she did and now you're just reneging out of jealousy. It's not an argument that'll carry the day in the end but the whole thing could get so drawn-out and ugly they could grind you down, force a settlement that still leaves you holding a pretty sizable bag."

"Maybe I'll just walk away from the house."

"If you're okay with that, why not do it now? Save yourself my legal fees."

Pilgrim cackled. "You don't want my money?"

"Not as much as some other people do, apparently."

Pilgrim blinked his eyes. He could feel the water building up. "And this Raymont Williams, this phony preacher, he walks away clean."

"I call it the Deadbeat Write-off. Meanwhile, for you, this could all get very expensive, particularly in addition to the other work you mentioned."

Pilgrim glowered, trying to shush her. He figured Corella had an ear pressed up to the door, trying to hear his business.

"Expensive is lying here doing nothing. I can't move. Don't mean I can't fight."

THAT NIGHT PILGRIM DREAMED he had his body back. He and Lorene were in the throes, the way it used to be—give some, not too much, take a little away then give it back till she's arching her spine and making that sound that made everything right. Damn near the only good he'd done his whole sorry life, pleasure that woman—that and turn himself into a quadriplegic piggy bank.

But no sooner did she make that gratified cry in his dream than the whole thing changed. He heard another sound, a low fierce hum, then the deafening broadside slam of the semi ramming his pickup, the fierce thrum of the diesel inches from his bleeding face through the shattered glass of his window, the scream of air brakes and metal against metal then the odd, hissing silence after. His head bobbing atop his twisted spine, body hanging limp in the shoulder harness. The smell of gas and smoldering rubber and that *tick-tick-tick* from the radiator that he mistook for dripping blood.

RAYMONT WILLIAMS, DRESSED IN pleated slacks and a cashmere V-neck, Italian loafers and silk socks, heard the doorbell ring and glanced down from a second story window. A fluffy little white fella, baggy suit, small hat, stood on the porch. Something wrong with this picture, he thought. White people in the neighborhood didn't come to visit.

Raymont lifted the window: "Yeah?"

The man backed up, gripping his hat so it wouldn't fall off as he tilted his head back to see who was talking. "Reverend Raymont Williams?"

No collar, Raymont thought, touching his throat. "You're who?"

"Name's William Montgomery. I live down the block. I received some of your mail. By mistake. The names, I guess." He tugged on the brim of his puny hat. "Kind of similar in a backwards sort of way."

"Shove it through the slot."

The man winced. "There's a bit of a snafu." He looked at the wad of mail in his hand, like it might catch fire. "One of the letters is certified, I signed by mistake. I don't know, I didn't look carefully, I just..." He scrunched up his face. "I called the post office. I have to get your signature, too, next to mine, then take the receipt down to the main office on Evans. It's a hassle, I realize—"

"That don't make sense."

"They were very specific. I'm truly sorry, reverend."

The hairs on Raymont's neck stood up. *You mocking me?* "Hold on." He closed the window, walked down the carpeted stairs to the entry. The crystal prisms on the chandelier refracted the sunshine streaming through the fanlight. In the dining room a bouquet of lilies and irises exploded from a crystal vase on the Hepplewhite side table. Lorene had this mania for Waterford lately, in addition to a number of other decorating obsessions. Out of control. They'd need to talk on that.

He flipped open the mail slot from inside. "Okay, slip it through."

The little man obliged. Raymont took the bundle of paper,

at which point the voice through the mail slot said, "Reverend Raymont Williams, a.k.a. Raymont Williams, a.k.a. Raymond White, a.k.a. Montel Dickson—you've been served with a summons and a complaint in accordance with state law and local rules of the California Superior Court. You must appear on the specified date or a default judgment may be filed against you. If you have any questions, you can call the number that appears on the summons."

Why you schemey little bug, Raymont thought. He pulled himself up, booming through the door: "How dare you. Coming here, full of hostile intent and subterfuge. I am a man of the cloth. What's the difficulty, tell me—the difficulty in simply ringing the bell like a decent man with honest business."

Beyond the door's beveled glass, the white man grinned, his eyes hard. He didn't look so fluffy now. "Yeah, right. Straight up, that's you." He turned and started down the steps, saying over his shoulder, "You're served."

Raymont threw the door open, came after him, one step, two. "You listen—"

The little man spun around. "Go ahead. I'll sue you for every cent you're worth."

Raymont cocked his head, perplexed. "Will you now?" He reached out, lifted William Montgomery or whoever the hell he was off his little white feet and tossed him down to the sidewalk. His head hit with a hollow, mean-sounding thunk. The man groaned, curled up, clutching his hat.

"Sue me for every cent I'm worth? Joke's on you."

The phone started ringing inside the house. Raymont slammed the door behind him, went to the hallway and picked up. He could hear Lorene, sobbing.

"So. Lemme guess. They got you at work."

"We got ten days—to *get out*. That's *my house*—"

"What did you do? What did you say?"

"I tried, Raymont, I swear. But he is a stubborn, spiteful—"

"You best try again, woman. Try harder. Try till that horizontal nigger sees the motherfucking light of God damn day."

"MR. BAXTER SAYS I'M to stay in the room this time."

Robert opened the bedroom door so Lorene could go in. She put away the fifty dollars she'd planned to pass along, tidied her hair, gathered herself. "Fine then." She strode in like a shamed queen.

Pilgrim's voice stopped her cold. "You come here to try to weasel your way into my good graces, don't bother. You got ten days to quit. You and that hustling no-count you taken in. The two of you, not out by then, sheriff kicks you out."

Lorene gathered her pride. "From the very beginning, Pilgrim, you promised—"

"Promises don't always keep, Lorene. You crossed the line."

Lorene sat down and tried to collect her thoughts. *Crossed the line.* Yes. And what an interesting world it became, across that line. The things you never thought you could have, right there. But here and now she was running out of options. Still, she reminded herself: *I know this man.*

With the nurse there she couldn't be as bold as the moment called for. All she could do was lean forward, tip her cleavage into view, bite her lip. "What is it you want, Pilgrim?"

MARGUERITE SANK BACK IN the chair and tapped her foot. "I don't agree with this."

"Not your place to agree or disagree."

"That's not entirely true. I can withdraw."

"Just find me another lawyer, not so particular."

"Mr. Baxter, it may not be my place, but you might want to think of your estate plan as way to take care of your loved ones, not settle scores."

"I want that kind of talk, I'll turn on Oprah."

"All right. Fine." Marguerite took the papers out of her briefcase. "I've drawn things up the way you asked. Both sets." She glanced up. "Are you all right?"

Pilgrim blinked. His face was wet. "Damn eyes, is all."

CORELLA CAME THAT EVENING to visit and found her father sleeping. His breathing was faint, troubled. She put her hand to his forehead. Cool. Clammy.

Hurry up and die, she thought.

He'd always made no secret of his feelings. If her mother was in the room, Corella did not exist. Children are baggage. How much time had she wasted, pounding her heart against his indifference—only to melt at the merest *Hey there, little girl.*

As fickle as the man could be, he still had it all over her mother. That woman was scandalous. Corella had tried to be gracious, turn a blind eye to the parade of men through that big old house—even this Raymont creature—but then the woman started spending money like a crack whore on holiday and Corella had to draw a line. Woman's gonna burn up my inheritance, she thought. That can't stand.

She pulled up a chair to wait until her father woke up. A manila envelope peeked out from under the bed covers. Carefully, she lifted it out. The lawyer's address label was on the front, with the notation: "Pilgrim Baxter—Estate Plan—DRAFT." About time he got to this, she thought.

Corella had earned her teacher's certificate just as the new governor was talking about taking pensions away and basing salaries on "merit"—meaning your career lay in the hands of bored kids cut loose by lazy parents. Schoolwork? Not even. Not when there's curb service for rock and herb on the street, Grand Theft Auto on the Gameboy, streaming porn on the web. The American dream. She was sorry for what had happened to her father but the money was luck and she'd need all she could muster. Otherwise the future just looked too grim.

She checked to be sure he was still dozing then opened the envelope quietly, removed the papers inside. There was a living trust, a will, some other legal documents captioned "Baxter v. Williams et al." Not like I don't have a right to see, she thought. He'll need me to make the calls, transfer accounts, consult with the accountants and all.

She read every page, even the boiler plate. By the time she was done her whole body was shaking.

RAYMONT, WEARING HIS PREACHER collar under a gray suit, stared out through the beveled glass of the Victorian's front door at Corella on the porch. Girl's nothing but a snitch for her father, he thought. He felt like telling her to just go away but Lorene hadn't come home the night before. He'd rattled around all night alone in their canopy bed, like a moth inside a lampshade, wondering if he shouldn't call the police. But, given his troubles, that could turn tricky. Besides, he figured she wasn't missing. She was hiding.

He cracked open the door. "Your mama's not around."

Corella had her hands folded before her, prim as a nun. "I didn't come to see her."

She might as well have thrown a rock. "Say that again?"

"Turns out, you and I have something in common." She looked him square in the eye. "We need to talk."

They sat in the kitchen, Raymont sipping Hennessey with a splash of Seven-Up, Corella content with tap water as she told him what she'd learned.

"The lawsuit and eviction remain in place—against you. Everything against my mother is dismissed in exchange for her cooperation and truthful testimony."

Girl sounds like a bad day on Court TV, he thought. "Your mama says I forced her into anything, that's a damn lie. I may have *suggested*—"

"She gets the house, too. He's quit-claiming it to her. But the debt comes with it."

Raymont shook his glass, the ice rattled. "There's his pound of flesh. Payments too steep. She can't keep up, they'll foreclose."

Corella shook her head. "She'll be able to hold them off for a while. And the insurance annuity that pays for my father's care? It has a cash payout when he dies. Half a million dollars. He's giving half of that to my mother to pay down the debt. That should make it manageable but still steep enough it'll feel—if I know my mother and father—like punishment."

Girl understands her blood, he thought, I'll grant her that. "And the other half—who gets that?"

Corella shook her head, a little flinch of outrage. "It goes to the nurse."

Raymont put down his drink. "The *bouncer*?"

"'For services rendered charitably, patiently and generously.'"

Corella seemed about to cry by there was ice in her voice too. "I get nothing."

"You got a half-sister floating around somewhere, too, am I right?"

He might as well have slapped her. "She doesn't deserve anything! Where has she been? What has she done?"

"Easy. Easy. I just—"

"The nurse is bad enough. I'm the one in the family who's been there. Every day, *every day*—"

"Fine. Agreed. Fair enough." Raymont juiced up his drink with a little more cognac. The girl was getting on his nerves and he needed to think. His mind boiled. "I'm gonna hire me a lawyer," he said. "A real junkyard dog. You best find yourself one too, girl, before this all gets finalized."

Corella stood up from the table. "You're missing the point."

LORENE LEFT THE HOTEL where she was hiding and arrived in Hunter's Point shortly after dinner to visit with Pilgrim. Robert let her in and said, "Mr. Baxter said you and him would be wanting some private time." She opened her purse, figuring they were back on the old payment schedule, but Robert said, "No need for that, m'am." He grabbed his hat, glanced at his watch and said, "I'll come back in an hour."

She inferred from his cheerfulness that Pilgrim had informed him of his good fortune. Once Pilgrim executed his documents, the former wrestler and part-time bouncer would stand to inherit a princely sum. Pausing at the window, she watched him flounce out to his beat-up car. He'll buy himself a new one first thing, she thought, something everyone will stare at. New car, new clothes, flash and trash, waste it all. But who's the bigger fool for that—him or Pilgrim?

She went into the bedroom and stood beside the bed. Pilgrim gazed up at her. "You look tired," he said.

She smiled grimly, thinking: You have no idea. Tired of pretending I feel for you. Tired of keeping up that charade just so I can have the one thing I want, my home and the things in it, a safe place as I grow old. Tired of watching you hang on to your miserable life with all its petty jealousy and resentment and hate. Tired of trying to convince myself I can do what you want. You think you can control my life and who I love, now and forever, even from beyond the grave. So yes. I'm tired.

It's always the devil, she thought, who shows us who we really are. She knew Raymont was evil, but so? Love is not a choice and who would want it if it was? He'd taught her things. Fortune favors the bold. No risk, no reward. She did not intend to waste that lesson. And there were hatreds and resentments of her own to abide.

"Come here," Pilgrim whispered. "Visit with me."

She stepped out of her shoes, lowered the bed, climbed on and straddled him, edging forward on her knees. Maybe you'll forgive me, she thought. Maybe not.

"Let me move this," she said, wrestling the pillow from beneath his head.

"Lorene, damn, careful—"

She clamped the pillow across his face and pressed down hard. The plump soft weight muffled his cries. Two minutes, she thought. That's how long they say it takes for old folks in nursing homes and Pilgrim lacked even that much strength. The killing would leave tiny red dots in his eyes but she would call her own doctor, not his, say he'd just stopped breathing. Her doctor would take her word, sign the death certificate before anyone was the wiser. And though Robert would be suspicious when he got back—Christ Almighty, he'd be out a quarter of a million dollars—he'd be in no position to make trouble. The police would see right through him. Besides, she made out no better than he did with Pilgrim dead and no documents signed—why would she kill him?

Her heart pounded and she was drenched with sweat by the time it was over. She couldn't bear to lift the pillow, see his face. She just leaned down, listened for sounds of breathing. Nothing.

From behind: "You just do what I think?"

Lorene spun around on the bed. Raymont stood in the doorway. Stranger still, Corella peeked out from behind him.

"We knew you'd be here," Raymont said. "We saw the nurse leave. Corella has a key."

Lorene held out her hand. "Help me down."

Raymont approached her like he thought she might turn into a bat but helped her as she climbed off Pilgrim's body. He caught her when she nearly fell. Her knees felt rubbery. She almost fainted.

"I couldn't go through with it," she said.

Puzzled, Raymont lifted the pillow. "You already did."

"No, I mean go through with what he wanted me to do. Turn against you." A shudder went through her and she began to weep softly. "I'm so sorry."

"It's all right, baby, stop." He stroked her face. "Don't fret. We got it all figured out."

"We?" She wiped her face.

"Corella and me. She's the one stands to inherit, she's the next of kin."

"But Cynthia—"

"To hell with Cynthia." It was Corella, holding herself so tight it looked like she might explode if she let go.

Raymont, more gently, said, "Anybody heard from this Cynthia? Anybody even know where she is?"

"St. Louis. Somewhere near—"

"No, Lorene." He grabbed her by the shoulders, shook her. "No. Listen to me. Corella and me, we've come to an understanding." He looked at Pilgrim's body, the face exposed now. Vacant. Still. "Corella's gonna file the probate. She'll say she heard some talk about another daughter, tried hard to find her, couldn't. We ransack this place, destroy any letters or anything else that might give us away, lead somebody to where she is. Hell, why can't we pretend she doesn't even exist?"

"What about the lawyer? The one he's been talking to. What if he's told her—"

"Why should she care? You pay her whatever she's owed, she'll go away, trust me. One thing I know, it's lawyers."

The next impulse took Lorene by surprise. She reached for Raymont's face, clamped her eyes shut and pressed her mouth so hungrily against his she thought, again, she might faint. A cold pulse ran through her, it felt like laughter. *He's dead*, she thought. *He's dead and I'm free and God help me but I have lived for this moment.*

WATCHING HER MOTHER GRAB the bogus preacher within inches of her father's corpse, Corella suffered a moment of clarity so searing she nearly got sick. Nothing would change, she realized. She'd be used. These two revolting people would get what they wanted then toss her aside. She was a tool. She was baggage.

Raymont had brought a gun in case Robert had to be

dealt with. Corella crept up behind him, reached inside his coat pocket.

Raymont tried to catch her by the arm, missed. "What you playin' at?"

Corella gripped the weapon with both hands, waving it back and forth, at Raymont, at Lorene, at Raymont. She was crying.

Raymont held out his hand. "Put that down." Then: "This was your idea, girl."

Corella fired. Lorene screamed as the bullet hit Raymont in the shoulder. He howled in pain, cursed, reached for the wound, said, "I'll kill you," through clenched teeth but then she fired again, this time aiming for his face. The round went through his eye. Lorene's screams grew piercing. Raymont tottered, reached for something that wasn't there, and slowly collapsed to the floor.

"My God, Corella, why, Lord, what—"

Corella raised the barrel till it pointed at her mother. "Quiet," she said, barely above a whisper, then fired. The bullet ripped through Lorene's throat. The second went straight through her heart.

ROBERT CAME BACK FROM the Philly cheese steak shop on Oakdale he liked, chewing gum to counter the smell of the greasy cheese and grilled onions on his breath. He found the door unlocked. Odd, he thought. Careless of me. Smokehounds could just waltz in.

He went straight for the bedroom, make sure all was well, and stopped in his tracks. A man he didn't recognize sat slumped against the wall, a bloody hole where one eye had been, another in his shoulder. Lorene lay in a heap beside the bed, ugly wounds on her chest and neck. And Mr. Baxter lay in his bed, motionless as a hunk of wood, eyes and mouth gaping.

Corella sat on the floor against the wall, clutching a pillow, staring at nothing. A pistol rested on the floor, not far from her feet.

"They killed him," she whispered. "I came in …" Her voice trailed away. She glanced up at Robert.

Robert's eyes bounced back and forth, the gun, Corella. "You?"

"They killed him," she said again. Practicing.

Robert studied her, then said, "It's all right. I understand."

He went to the bedside, checked to make sure Pilgrim was dead, then checked the other two as well. From a box beside the bed he withdrew a vinyl glove, slipped it on his hand.

"You hurt?" he asked Corella, walking over to the gun, picking it up.

She shook her head. Then, looking up into his face, she said, "He never signed those documents, you know. You get nothing."

Robert crouched down in front of her. "Sometimes it's not about the money." With one hand he forced her mouth open, with the other he worked the barrel in. "Sometimes it's just the right thing to do."

TWO DAYS AFTER the funerals, Marguerite Johnstone sat in her office, meeting with Pilgrim's surviving daughter, Cynthia. She'd traveled from Hannibal, Missouri, for the services. Her mother had stayed behind.

"Your father had me draft two estate plans," Marguerite explained, "one he executed the last time I met with him, the other he was saving."

Cynthia tilted her head quizzically. "Saving?"

She was quite different from Corella, Marguerite thought. She had Midwestern manners, played the cello, wore Chanel. More to the point, she was Korean. Or half Korean, anyway.

"He wanted to see how his ex-wife followed through on certain promises. Obviously, that's all moot now."

Cynthia shuddered. "It sounds so terrible."

The night of the murders, the police received reports of gunfire in the neighborhood but that was like saying it was dark at the time. No one could pinpoint where the shots came from till Robert called 9-1-1. The detectives working the case had their doubts about his story but he'd held up under questioning and passed his gunshot residue test. Besides, the new mayor was lighting bonfires up their buttholes—their phrase—because of their pitiful clear rate on the dozens of drive-bys and gang hits in that neighborhood. Last thing they wanted to do was waste time on a domestic. As it sat, the case had a family angle and a murder-suicide tidiness to it and that permitted them to close it out with a clear conscience. If justice got served in the bargain, fabulous.

"The documents your father actually executed leave everything to you. The Excelsior house has so little equity and is so heavily leveraged I'd consider just walking away. Let the lenders fight over it. The Hunter's Point lot—forget the house—might bring fifty thousand. That's a guess, we'll have it appraised. That leaves the cash payout from the annuity."

Cynthia looked up. "And that would be?"

"In the ballpark of half a million."

The girl's eyes ballooned. "I had no idea. I mean, my father and I, we weren't in touch. My mother, she's become more and more … traditional. She felt ashamed. She and my father weren't married and they—" Her cheeks colored. She wrung her hand-kerchief in her lap. "I wrote from time to time but never visited. Not even after his accident. Corella was the one—"

"It wasn't Corella's decision to make. It was your father's property. That's the way it works."

"But—"

"From the way he talked about it, I gathered it was precisely the fact you didn't hang around, waiting for him to die, that made him feel benevolent toward you."

Cynthia pondered that, then shrugged. "It still feels a little like stealing, to be honest."

"You can't steal a gift, not under the law anyway." Margue-rite glanced at the clock, reminding herself: billable hours. "Are there any questions you'd like to ask?"

Cynthia put her chin in her hand and tapped her cheek with her forefinger. Too cute, Marguerite thought. The innocence was beginning to grate.

"I hope this doesn't sound crass," Cynthia said finally, "But when will I get my check?"

Marguerite bit her lip to keep from grinning. Families, death and money, she thought. Didn't matter your race or creed—or how far away you lived—the poison always bubbles up from somewhere, often long before the dear departed's body grows cold.

"That depends on the insurance company administering the annuity. Why?"

Cynthia shrugged. "Nothing. I was thinking about maybe traveling." She blushed again. "It's my boyfriend's idea, actually."

Interesting, Marguerite thought. "'Travel is a privilege of the young.' I read that somewhere. Why didn't your boyfriend come with you?"

"He lives here. We just met." The color in her cheeks deepened. "It's sudden, I realize, and he's really not my type but I've felt lonely here and he's very kind. He introduced himself at the church service. You may know him, actually, he took care of my father."

Bobby the Prop Buys In

IT WAS MIDNIGHT AND Bobby Roper sat in the office of the Eucalyptus Room watching his boss, Sal Lazzarini, run a tape on the week's damage. Sundays, Sal closed at eleven to tally things up, kicking out the last of the weekend losers. They'd sit there at the sucker tables till daybreak if you let them, pissing away a year's worth of alimony, the balloon payment on the mortgage, the kid's tuition. It hurt, Sal told Bobby, giving them the boot—a card room's bread and butter, types like that—but you had to run the numbers sometime.

Sal squinted in the lamplight at his desk as he punched the figures into his adding machine. He was a beefy man, gone jowly and soft-muscled at sixty, but still imposing, even sitting down. He had impeccably combed white hair and a broad pockmarked face that withered up, eyes narrowing to slits, when he inhaled from his cigarette.

"Little skinks are stealing me blind." He shook his head, studying the total for the cage drawer shortages from his cashiers. "Amounts are insane."

Bobby sat on the big white sofa across from Sal's desk—the only employee left, the others having long ago headed home. He could speak freely. "So ax somebody. Make an example."

"Where you been? Last month alone, two okay? Sent the little thieves packing. Guess who hired them back."

He meant his partner, Phil Vogel. Phil provided the capital for the card room, Sal the gambling know-how, a not uncommon arrangement. It brought with it not uncommon problems. Phil came from old Hillsborough money, the family black sheep, and like most guys of that stripe he was scared down deep. He tried to cover up by playing the big shot but he knew it was all a lie and so he drank. The drink, it made him an easy play.

"Show up in a leather skirt and a Wonder bra," Sal said, "tease your hair like cotton candy, Phil can't feel for you fast enough."

Sal turned to the floor shorts next. From time to time the chip girls snuck loans from their aprons to gamblers, hoping by shift's end to make it all back with "interest."

"You try and tell 'em, guy's already on a downslide when he hits you up. Luck don't change in here. It's what the place is for." Sal made a little moaning sigh as he licked his pencil tip then entered the sums in his ledger. "Of course, I say that, make them cover the shortage, I'm a prick, right? Old Phil, he's all, 'Don't cry, baby cakes.'"

Last, Sal ran the tally on the bum chits and dubious checks Phil had okayed. Tearing off the tape, he tossed it across the desk. "That's twenty-three grand right there." The scroll of white paper fluttered like a tiny kite through Bobby's fingers. "One week, understand? The chits are fucking gone, okay? Be a miracle we ever make good on them. And sixty to eighty percent of the checks gonna sail right back NSF or with a stop order." Sal uncapped the fifth of Cutty Sark he kept in his desk and freshened his glass. "That's my partner. Him and that pack of wind merchants he calls friends." He swirled the scotch in his glass, studying it like it helped him think. "Sick of it, Bobby. Only a matter of time before he fucks us all. Which gets us back to me and you." He scratched his stubbled cheek with his knuckles and sat back in his chair, rocking a little, away from the lamplight. "So—got something for me?"

Bobby unbuttoned his sport coat, squirming forward in his seat. He'd been dreading this part. "Sal, you know, that's what I've been meaning—"

"You ain't got it."

"I've got most."

"Most? What's most?"

"My player's bank, in the vault there, it's eighteen."

"*Eighteen?*" Sal, incredulous, patted his waxy white hair. "You come here to insult me with eighteen?"

"I've got the rest."

"On you?"

"Yeah, well, here's the deal—"

"You gonna tell me eighteen is *it*? Total?"

"The other two's promised to me."

Sal cackled. "Promised. Christ. I love that." Then it hit him. "*Two?* You think twenty's gonna—"

"Sal, hear me out, okay? You said—"

"Twenty? Never."

"Sal, don't take that tone. It's not right."

"Fuck right. It's fifty a point, always has been. Where you been, the eighties?"

"Sal, there's no need to yell, okay? I'm sitting right here."

"You think I don't know my own damn numbers?"

"Look, let me tell you the deal."

"Midnight's the god damn deadline, Bobby, I told you. Partnership agreement spells it out. Gotta cut off shares some point, it's the legalities."

"Sal, I realize, yeah, yeah, but listen, okay?" Bobby hated what he had to say next. Not because it wasn't true. It just made him feel weak. "Trink, the asthma, she's had these doctor bills you wouldn't believe."

Sal stiffened, cocking his head. "Shut up."

"Sal?"

"I said shut the fuck up." He squinted, cocking his ear toward the door as he stubbed out his smoke. In a whisper: "You don't hear that?"

Bobby leaned in, whispering back, "Hear what?"

Sal shimmied open the top drawer of his desk, withdrew a small, nickel-plated revolver and checked the cylinder for live rounds. "Stay put." He nodded toward the door behind his desk, leading from his office out the back way into the employee parking lot. "Anything goes bad, you run, understand? Don't play hero."

Sal struggled from his chair and edged across the room. The pistol looked toylike in his hand but even so Bobby eyed it like it might suddenly fly up like a bat and sail across the room straight at him. In the doorway Sal craned his neck to peer down the dark hall out toward the cage.

"I'll be right back."

Bobby sat mesmerized, watching Sal disappear. Five seconds passed. Ten.

"Hey! Who the hell—"

A gunblast erupted in the hallway. A deafening tinny echo rippled along the walls. Bobby dropped from his chair to the floor, covering his ears, ashamed at his cowardice. Straightening up but still on his knees, he called out, "Sal! You okay?"

A stranger entered the doorway—medium build, medium height, nothing to distinguish him but what he wore: ratty black turtleneck under a limp brown suit, ski mask hiding his face. He had to tip his head back and a little to the side to see out the eyeholes, the mask on so crooked. He held a gun, too. It looked big in his hand, not like Sal's. Bobby couldn't take his eyes off it.

He lifted his hands. "Please. Listen. I'm just here, you know, I can't ... " The words trailed away. He had no idea what to beg for, not with so little faith it would matter. And yet as that first wave of terror broke he suffered an eerie sense of familiarity. The way the man carried himself. The eyes for sure.

SIX HOURS EARLIER, Bobby'd stood at the stove in his apartment, begging a kettle of water to boil and listening as Trink tore through the bathroom medicine cabinet and vanity drawers, desperate for an inhaler she hadn't sucked dry.

Bobby called out, "Trink, Trink! What'd you wear last night? Check the pockets!"

Easy now, he thought. You freak, she freaks, the whole thing spins outta control. From the bathroom her raspy breath bit like a saw down her throat and lungs. She would've screamed if she'd had the air. Bottles crashed as she tried to exhale, couldn't.

The carbon dioxide was building up, the toxicity in her blood. Couple of minutes she'd black out. Worse if he didn't get her to Emergency in time.

The teakettle whistled and Bobby snatched it from the stovetop, burned his hand, dropped the thing. "No. Fuck. No." He grabbed a towel, dodging barefoot the puddle of scalding water as he picked up the kettle and shook it, checking to see how much remained. Spinning back to the sink, he doused the coffee grounds in the drip filter, splashing gritty shmutz everywhere. Just enough for a good half cup, he thought. Plenty strong that way. Think positive.

He stumbled to the bathroom. Trink sat in a heap on the floor, clutching the edge of the sink with a pale, skeletal hand, chest heaving as she sucked on a small silver canister of Albuterol. She'd used up all her Asthmacort, and her dependency on the Albuterol was the latest turn of bad luck. Before that it had been the mold infiltration in the apartment walls, an endless bout of flu they'd passed back and forth since Halloween, a case of thrush in her mouth from the inhalants. Then, the topper, the elevator—two months now, the thing was locked between floors. You complained to the landlord, he'd just say, "Blame rent control," and slam down the phone. They lived on the seventh floor. Might as well be the top of Mt. Sutro. For all intents and purposes, Trink was a prisoner.

Bobby knelt beside her as she pressed the plunger on her inhaler one more time, sucking deep on the spray. Dark patches rimmed her eyes, which were spent and glazed.

"You strong enough to walk to the kitchen, or you want me to bring the coffee in?"

She shook her head, like she couldn't believe he'd ask such

a thing, twitching from the pain in her diaphragm. Her breath came in quick shallow tremors and she rubbed her throat.

"I'll just be a second." He collected the half-cup of coffee from the kitchen sink and hurried back. In a mock accent, vaguely Transylvanian, he said, "Black like night, strong like bull." Trying to joke, turn the mood around.

She'd inherited most of her features from her dad, her poor constitution and bone white skin from her mom. Tiny, with birdlike legs and arms, she spread oddly wide at the hips, square in the can, small-breasted, with an upturned nose and a sloping jaw that gave her a strangely vixenish underbite. Her lips were plump, curving wickedly at the edges, and she had the kind of wintry blue eyes that could stop you dead. Her pixie haircut accentuated how small she was to where, in her cotton briefs and tank top, barefoot, gasping for breath on the cold hard floor, she looked like a dying child. Except for the tattoos.

"Get me the aspirin." She fluttered her hand toward the medicine cabinet. Bobby obliged—it would mean she'd taken every conceivable measure to stop the attack—and she popped three tablets with the coffee. Settling back against the wall, legs tucked up under her, she gathered a few even breaths then said, "It's not fair. I eat like nothing that's not green. I cut out the sugar. Cut out the salt, the wheat. Well, most of the wheat. No wine, no whiskey, just vodka."

Bobby smiled. Yes, well, ahem, he thought. You still smoke.

"You do what they tell you," she said, "you should catch some slack."

She'd started smoking at age eight. Her three older brothers were out in the peat mounds that belonged to the greenhouse behind the schoolyard. Trink—Jennifer Trinka, third grade,

Star of the Sea Elementary—snuck up, spotted them passing the Marlboro pack around.

"I'm telling," she hissed, then fled.

They ran after her, forced her to the ground and made her smoke with them and said if she told on them, they'd tell on her. Did that every day for a month, till they didn't need to hold her down anymore. Two years passed before she caught on to what a lame threat they'd made and by then she had a half-pack-a-day habit, ten years old. The asthma kicked in not long after when she hit puberty; she had a two-pack habit by then. She'd been flirting with suffocation ever since, working cocktail, chip girl, rooms hazed with smoke.

With the heel of her hand she wiped at one eye then the other. "Not fucking fair."

"No, it's not." What could he say? She was his girl.

"I don't want to die in this hellhole, Roper. Okay?"

"I'm working on it."

An old pit boss of Bobby's from his Reno days had settled in Minden, gotten in touch, said he had a housing deal. Come up with thirty grand, he said, he could work them into a condo meant for the casino staff, rig the financing through the union. Nothing magnificent, three rooms and a kitchen, but Bobby had no credit—name a gambler who did—he couldn't be choosy. And it was high desert. Good for asthmatics.

Bobby'd been doing all right getting the money together till Trink's string of therapeutic sidetracks and sudden disasters this past year—acupuncture, allergy tests, a pneumonia booster, then the thrush and the mold and the flu and four trips to Emergency where they amped her up on adrenaline so bad they had to monitor her for heart attack, after which she felt like the nurses had gone at her with hammers. And given her asthma, insurance?

Forget about it. Every single payout for care or meds came out of pocket, full price. She couldn't work anymore. With the elevator out, couldn't even leave the apartment. Bobby was on his own, down to his last eighteen grand, kept in his player's bank at the Eucalyptus Room. He'd lose that too if he didn't do something.

It was why he'd jumped on Sal's offer, decided to buy in to his new secret partnership. He needed a chance to score big.

Trink pursed her lips, chest shivering as she exhaled. "Just once in my life, Roper, I'd love not to have to think about my next breath, you know?"

BOBBY HAD GONE TO COLLEGE and he'd studied enough Psych to know what was going on. The imprint, so to speak. He was drawn to wounded birds: Women who were self-tortured victims of their own poor judgment. Like his mother.

He'd been an only child, she a single mom, and they'd moved around a lot. Bobby'd only known his father through photographs. He'd been handsome with an effortless grace about him, generous with a smile and never seeming ill at ease in front of the camera. At least, until Bobby's mother got pregnant. The snapshots ended then, along with the marriage. By the time Bobby was old enough to understand what a father was, his was nothing more than a rumor told to him when his mother drank.

She called him a sociopath or, if she was feeling clever, a born salesman. He'd liked his games—horses, cards—liked his liquor and his girls and he'd disappear for days, weeks sometimes, then come back smelling of drink and gamy sweat and another woman's bed. When he left, he said he'd never wanted a family and how cruel could she be, bringing a kid into the world when she knew that.

It took twenty years for his mother to finally drag her heart out of its box to meet somebody new. Ralph Stoudemire: he brokered professional liability coverage and taught ballroom dancing. The dancing, it was like Bobby's mom had been reborn.

"Come visit us, Bobby, couldn't you? Your mother's happy for once—do you understand?"

Bobby met them for drinks at the Embarcadero Hyatt in San Francisco. Bobby's mom, the chain-smoking English teacher, wore lipstick and eyeliner and rouge, first time in years, and a cocktail dress, high heels. Ralph wore a blue blazer and brown slacks, reeking of cologne and breath mints. It was like a prom date, the light in their eyes when they sat together, the giggles, the furtive little pinches. Then the hotel orchestra struck up "Begin the Beguine." Ralph shot to his feet, pulling her with him, and they were gone. The dark dance floor shimmered from a recent waxing and their reflections flickered beneath them as they swirled and stopped and circled, defying gravity for a little while. Not long enough. Six months later, after Ralph emptied all her accounts and disappeared, Bobby's mom climbed out of the bottle just long enough to say, "That's it. I'm done. Men leave, they take everything and they don't come back. I'm only so brave."

And there you had it, Bobby thought. He'd both mimicked and defied the example of the men in his mother's life. Admiring their swagger, their cutthroat charm, their worldliness, but bettering them by being smarter, stronger, loyal. He hadn't left Trink, he'd stayed. He'd taken nothing from her. On the contrary, he'd given all he had.

Bobby knew he owed some of that to Sal. They shared an odd simpatico, all the more strange because of the vast difference between them. Bobby'd been little more than a smart ass with a talent for cards when he'd shown up at the Eucalyptus Room. Sal made a gambler, a man, out of him—not so much because of anything he'd said or done, just by example. And that, Bobby suspected, made Sal the kind of man he'd been secretly hunting for all his life—not a father figure, but not one of his mother's mistakes, either.

BOBBY UNDERSTOOD PERFECTLY WELL that the buy-in for Sal's offer was fifty, but he figured if he could just scratch up an extra two, show up with twenty even, Sal might negotiate. And in three months, the way Sal had pitched the deal, Bobby could turn the twenty into thirty, cash out, send his old pit boss the down and get Trink where she needed to be, up in the thin cool air, the sunbleached heat, the high desert. But he still needed another two grand. That was where Eddie Mott came in.

Bobby had to cab it to the Richmond District where Eddie lived because his own car had died, and he couldn't throw good money after bad right now. Eddie's wife, a Korean named Claudia, opened the door, all five feet of her. She wore a washed-out housedress, hair in rollers, gazing up at Bobby through smudged glasses. There was no explaining gamblers and their wives, Bobby realized, but he'd always thought Eddie had stooped particularly low.

Claudia spoke in short, shrill bursts of sound, like a swim coach with his whistle. "Eddie not here! Mother's house!" She gave Bobby the address then slammed the door.

The place was clear across town in Echo Park. It cost Bobby forty-three bucks with tip to get there by cab, and he figured it'd be wise to hit up Eddie for that as well. He was down to fifty-six dollars pocket money.

The taxi let him out in front of a stucco duplex. Mud-colored stains fingered down from the rain gutters and mold speckled the window ledges. Every house on the narrow street looked as bad if not worse. A brisk wind blew trash down the sidewalks.

Bobby tried the door, discovered it open. "Eddie?"

Passing through the doorway, he entered a museum of motherly kitsch glazed with dust. The place stank of mildew, the windows all closed tight, plus a heavy stench of gas. But there was a foul human smell, too.

Bobby found Eddie in the kitchen, perched like a toad on a tiny wood foot stool, staring at a sun-faded flower-print bed sheet covering a lumpy shape. The odors were worse in here. The oven door stood open. Duct tape sealed the windows and still hung tattered along the edges of the doorway.

"Eddie, hey," Bobby whispered, thinking: Good God.

Eddie glanced just once at Bobby, nodded, then returned his gaze to the washed out bedsheet.

"I had to move her. They're gonna get pissed, the cops I mean, but fuck them. I had to."

Eddie was possibly the most placid person Bobby knew, but he sensed something dark, something hostile, dragging at his voice like an undertow. Bobby slipped up behind, squeezed Eddie's shoulder. "Christ, Eddie, this is, I don't know, terrible."

Eddie nodded solemnly. He was a hulking, soft, plain man, with a wardrobe from Sears—gray, beige, white, more gray—and a face memorable solely due to his horn-rimmed glasses. His life consisted of repairing computers in his garage and playing cards.

"She called out of the blue, left a message. 'I'm going away. Don't worry if I don't answer the phone.' That was it. Her voice, I don't know, I just had a feeling."

Bobby tried to picture it, a mother calling like that. He felt scared suddenly about his own mom and made a mental note to phone her. It had been a while.

"People don't die the way you think, Bobby. Smell that?" Eddie's nostrils flared and he winced, pushing his glasses up the bridge of his nose. "Not the gas, the other thing. I cleaned up most of it but, you know, the muscles relax. Not right, cops find her like that."

"Respect, Eddie, it's important." Bobby felt desperate for air. "Hey, listen. This probably isn't the best time, but I—"

"Her head in the fucking oven, Bobby. It's a message. I don't feel despair here, Bobby, I feel anger."

Yeah, but whose, Bobby wondered. "Don't take this on yourself, Edster. Old folks, they get depressed."

"Sixty-two, Bobby. Just sixty-two. That's young."

"Too young, Eddie. You're right, what can I say? Listen—"

"Gotta admit, can't say I cared for her all that much, you know? Used my old man up like a bag of peas. Me, I was just the errand boy. But you know, today of all days, she's my mother, and what ain't right, ain't right."

Bobby was kneading Eddie's shoulders now, working them like a weight room trainer. "Eddie, Eddie, I understand. Totally. The human condition, it's supremely wack. Now, like I said, this ain't the best time I realize—"

A loud knock sounded at the front door. Bobby spotted two cops venturing in through the living room.

"Anybody? Hello?"

Like that, Eddie shot to his feet. "Look who decided to show the fuck up!" He hitched up his belt and lurched into the living room. "That all my mother means to you guys? Just another yeah-yeah-yeah?"

"Sir," the lead cop said, raising his hand. "Back up."

No, Bobby thought. This can't happen. Out of the corner of his eye he spotted Eddie's key ring on the kitchen counter as the voices in the living room started to boil. Eddie's headed for lockup, Bobby thought, what good's his car to him. He snatched the keys, shoved them in his pocket, as the same cop shouted, "I meant what I said. Back the fuck up, fat man, or we do the dance."

THE NEXT FEW HOURS dragged by like a Swedish movie. The cops wouldn't let Bobby go till they could write out a report and Eddie just kept cycling through paranoid fits of guilty rage and sad-sack crying jags, at one point mewling in misery on one cop's shoulder, same cop he took a swing at not thirty seconds later. That was when they put the cuffs on and called for backup. When Bobby tried to suggest that everybody just, you know, chill, he got told to shut up and sit tight or he'd be joining his friend in stir.

Bobby slinked off to the kitchen table where he sat and chewed his thumbnail, watching the hands on the clock while more and more cops showed up. Even the Neptune Society got there before Bobby could finally steal one of the cops into a corner and talk him into jotting down enough so he could leave.

"Eddie, Eddie, you be strong!" Bobby waved goodbye through the crowd of uniforms. Backing into the living room, he collided with the crematorium's gurney. It scared a little yelp out of him and he spun around, apologizing to the bored tech who just sat there on the couch, paging through an ancient copy of *The Potrero Bingo Beacon*.

Out on the street, Bobby spotted Eddie's car, blocking a

driveway. It was one of the new VW Bugs—white, of course, dullest color they had, and automatic, not a stick. Check it out, he thought: One of the cops had written Eddie a ticket. That was cold. Bobby snatched the ticket from under the windshield wiper, tossed it into the gutter then got behind the wheel and drove off as fast as he could. He'd tell Eddie later that he'd only borrowed the Bug because Eddie himself insisted—so Bobby could come around the county lockup later, bail him out, drive him home. Eddie'd be too drunk from his own mood swings to remember for sure what he had and hadn't said the past few hours.

Bobby gassed the Bug's throaty little turbo through Vistacion Valley and up the rim of hills connecting Candlestick with the San Bruno range, dropping down again at Oyster Point and following the Bayshore Freeway south. The Eucalyptus Room sat along the briny mud flats lining the Dumbarton Bridge approach. He pulled into the parking lot just before the ten o'clock closing. Okay, he thought, no two grand. But it wasn't like Eddie refused. That's what he'd tell Sal. Just a temporary setback. You know, bad luck.

BOBBY'D MOVED BACK to the Bay Area two years earlier, after leaving Chico State without a degree and working the tables in Reno for a while. His mother had moved to Albuquerque for a total lifestyle makeover so San Francisco seemed like a whole new city. No dreary echoes, no morbid shadows.

He quickly found his way to the peninsula south of town and marveled at how much money rolled through the card rooms. There among the suburbs with their car lots and strip malls and office parks you had players with more attitude than card sense and a careless abandon when it came to their own incomes.

Bobby ended up favoring the Eucalyptus Room, Sal Lazzarini's place, down in East Palo Alto. It had a reputation for hard play at the sixty/one-twenty tables and was rumored to draw a rough crowd. But all that was fine with Bobby. He'd learned to play poker with sawed-off roughnecks—long-haulers, skip tracers, meth-head carpenters and boozy, chain-smoking barbers—the kind of creatures who inhabited the slummy neighborhoods his mother could afford to live in. Those guys would have fit in like furniture at the Eucalyptus Room. Besides, there was this chip girl there. Her name was Jennifer Trinka.

She wore her hair longer then, halfway down her back in long permed curls. It set off the soft smooth whiteness of her skin and the hard cold blue of her eyes. Boyish in the chest, she emphasized her legs instead, wearing kinky heels and shameless skirts. Guys at the tables couldn't love her enough. Bobby knew he couldn't just make his play from the floor, like every other mope. He needed status.

He hung around, doing the rail bird bit, making idle chat with the help and hoping to team up with someone, play partners at a high spread table. It was the only way to make real money in a room like that. You had fools getting hosed at Texas Hold 'Em and Low Ball, forty hands per hour. Meanwhile, across the room, Asians threw insane amounts of money away at Pai Gow and Pan Nine, thrilling Sal since the house had a stake in every ante and winning pot.

As Bobby settled in over time, he seemed to get along okay with folks—he had a talent for that, getting along—but couldn't quite get that second leg over, especially with Sal. Then one night, Trink sidled up, smiling like she knew something he didn't.

"Mr. Lazzarini would like a word."

Bobby followed her back to the office, memorizing the

tiny waist, the rippling black hair, the pendulum action of her strangely boxy tush, marveling at the strong stockinged legs with her tattoos peeking through the mesh. At the office door she turned like a game show hostess and gestured him inside.

"You joining us?" He tried not to sound too hopeful.

She didn't answer, but he noticed that her smile lingered as she walked away.

It was the first time Bobby'd been in the office, first time alone with Sal for that matter. They'd traded nods and smiles on the floor, but never spoken beyond small talk. But Bobby already knew he liked Sal, respected him. He seemed unbothered by doubt, as though thought was just a kind of action—you sized up a man asking for credit, you tallied odds—and beyond that reflection was pointless, counterproductive, even dangerous.

The office, small and plain, smelled like an ashtray, hugger-mugger with display cases and file cabinets piled high with tottering stacks of tally sheets. Sal sat behind his cluttered desk. The only other place to sit was a sofa made of white naugahyde that brought to mind Las Vegas in the fifties. Somebody had to kill a lot of Cadillacs to make this thing, Bobby thought, sitting down. He offered a deferential smile and waited to be spoken to.

Sal, a pair of cheaters slung low on his nose, jotted figures in a ledger. "You like it here," he said finally, not looking up. "The card room, I mean."

"Very much."

"See you a lot around the tables, checking things out."

"Yeah." The phrase caught Bobby's ear funny: *checking things out*. He leaned forward, whispering for comic effect, "That's not a problem, right?"

He cracked a grin that Sal, glancing up finally, did not return.

"There's some people out there think you're a cop. Any truth in that?"

Bobby's throat closed up. He dressed straight, not showy— slacks and sport jackets, Oxford button-downs. It was easier to get marks at the tables to trust you that way. He hadn't thought it also might make him look narky. And yeah, he'd been hanging around, trying to get folks to like him. Trust him.

"I mean, it's okay if you are." Sal studied him, taking his time. "I don't mind if cops hang out. Kinda hope they do, to be honest. Anything crooked goes down in my store, I wanna know about it."

Horseshit, Bobby thought. There was talk two city council members were silent partners in the club, and that drove the local cops nuts. They saw the Eucalyptus Room as a flash point for trouble. Beyond the hard play and rumors of time advances at the tables, you had chip girls not just sneaking loans but dealing crack out of their aprons; known bookies and fences waltzing around like kings; a pair of Filipino bank robbers who confessed their heists were driven by gambling losses at the Pai Gow tables. Two stolen cars had been found in the parking lot just last week. Some sorry shmuck had been kidnapped after winning ten grand and another'd been robbed and knifed.

Finding his voice finally, Bobby said, "I'm not a cop."

Sal rose to his feet behind his desk and stuck out his meaty hand. His eyes said: *Time will tell*. "Pleasure talking finally."

BACK ON THE FLOOR, Bobby hunted up a house prop named Gap Quattrone. Props were players staked by the house to team up on suckers, hold them at the tables and keep them losing. Bobby'd sat there one night watching Gap and his partner take a car salesman for twenty-two grand over fifteen straight hours of play. The code they used was primitive, knee knocks and ear pulls so obvious they could've been little league coaches signaling from the dugout. Bobby found Gap—the name was short for Gaspar—standing at a sink in the Men's, combing his wavy blond hair.

"Join me outside for a smoke?"

It was a clear spring night, the racket from Highway 101 unusually loud, like always after a rain. Bobby lit a cigarette for himself, held the match out for Gap, too, and tried to think of how to begin. Gap cupped his hands to the flame, looking almost perfect in its flickering light.

Gap could have been a Hollywood actor—not a star, but one of those faces you always recognize but can seldom put a name to. The guy, you'd say. Which guy? You know, *the guy*. The too-slick weatherman whose wife walks out first scene in the movie. The psycho killer's hip-but-not-hip-enough neighbor. First bad guy in the Florida prison break the alligators drag under. Gap looked good, not great, but he did things, even little things—a wink for the cocktail waitress, a drag from his cigarette—like he knew you were watching. And you were.

Finally, sensing the moment was right, Bobby said, "Look, I know you're playing partners. The guys you team with are a joke. And your code's so gross my grandmother's canasta group could nail you. People think I'm a cop. Well, tell you what. I'll teach you a code nobody will catch, and if I'm a cop that's entrapment, so I've just given you an ironclad defense. What do you say?"

Things improved after that. Gap picked up fast on Bobby's routine—fanning his cards left or right depending on whether he intended to stay in or fold, using stage business with his chips or his cigarettes or his coffee cup to signal ace, king, queen, jack, and how many of each, changing the code around several times a night. Bobby even taught him how to deal seconds and from the bottom. They practiced together till their hand movements possessed the required subtlety and they could read each other without needing to look straight on.

On Gap's good word Sal finally changed his take on Bobby, staking him with house money then taking half of what he and Gap won on any night. Business was good. The Nevada houses were closing their poker operations due to the competition from the California card rooms. The casinos never much liked the poker crowd anyway; they generated little side action and tended to prey on the tourists. And so the money started drifting in to the Eucalyptus Room, some players smarter than others, but few of them smart enough. Even the ones who caught on backed down once they realized getting serious meant dealing with Sal.

There were still those around the club who called Bobby "professor" because he'd been to college, or "junior" because of his youth, hoping to somehow undermine his growing bond with Sal. And when it got out that he'd majored but never earned a degree in English, same subject his mother had taught in high school, the badgering turned heartless. He could hardly have done worse studying interpretive dance. In some ways it worked to his advantage, the mockery; the suckers didn't take him seriously and it made them easier to play. But there was a bite, a vengefulness to some of it that made his deepening bond with Sal crucial. Sal suffered no fools. His regard for Bobby meant standing. Protection. And an extra advantage came with that—with Bobby squarely in Sal's good graces, Trink finally took him seriously.

They started with after-shift breakfasts: Bobby would sit there listening to the latest version of the Perils of Jennifer Trinka and watch as she sent her scrambled eggs back to the kitchen time and time again, till they came back rubbery, like gum erasers. "There's only one thing runny I want in my mouth," she'd tell him and he couldn't hear it enough. Six weeks later they were living together. He'd never done that before. Never bought jewelry for a woman, either, or sat on the toilet and watched as she lathered and shaved her legs in the tub. Never shared a beer for Saturday breakfast or had a woman tell him, as he lay with her in bed, "You can do anything you want. Just give me some warning if you're gonna hit me, okay?"

But Bobby wasn't a hitter. It was all he could do to oblige her request that he hold her down during sex. One more legacy of the schoolyard bullying she took from her brothers when she was eight: She liked to struggle with him on top of her. Same way she liked to smoke.

ONE NIGHT SAL CAME UP, gestured Bobby and Gap away from their game. Once he had them off the floor, he said, "Come with me, okay? I need somebody to see this."

They drove to a nearby watering hole called the Eight Ball—a jump joint, like most bars in East Palo Alto. Phil Vogel sat alone on his stool, sagging like his spine had turned to putty and staring into his glass. Crumpled bills, too many, sat in plain view, inviting trouble. The bartender, who'd called Sal at the club, nodded as though to say, Get him out of here. The other customers, some of whom wore prison tats or gang colors, made no secret of their curiosity. They sipped Hennessey and Coke or bottled malt liquor, prowled around the pool table or chewed on plastic straws at the tables near the back, eyeing Sal and Gap and Bobby like the Marx Brothers had just shown up.

Sal came up behind his partner and leaned close. "Time to knock off, Phil. Let's go, while the going's good."

Phil shot a screw-you look at Sal in the mirror, not straight on, then gestured to the bartender for another. Sal glanced up at the bartender and shook his head.

"You think I'm joking? Come on. We'll drive you back to the club."

Sal slipped his hand under Phil's arm but the sad fat drunk broke free, stumbling off his stool in a wild-limbed stagger then spinning around. He fumbled in his pocket for something. "Where would you be, huh? Without me. Where?" He pulled from his pocket what he wanted, finally—a femmy little .22, wiggling it in the air. He looked like he wanted to cry, which was what Bobby felt like doing, too, once he saw the pistol sailing around like that. Didn't matter how small it was, Bobby hated guns. It was almost a phobia, like some people with spiders or heights. You could talk a man out of almost anything, you did it right, but a gun, it just does what it was built for. It tore open flesh. It ripped arteries and muscle apart. He doesn't even have to want to, Bobby thought. Accidents happen.

Sal didn't so much as glance at the weapon, just stared into his partner's rheumy eyes. "You sad old faggot." He turned to the bartender. "Call the cops on this piece of crap." Then, turning to Gap and Bobby: "Let's get back to work."

Bobby stood frozen in place, still staring at the gun. Gap took notice and whispered, "Come on," grabbing Bobby's sleeve. "Never let jigs see you're scared."

The bartender called out, "I ain't callin' no cops on his ass.

Don't need that kind of trouble. You haul his sorry drunk butt on outta here."

But Sal just kept walking. Bobby couldn't follow him fast enough and Gap took up the rear, making sure Phil didn't shoot and nobody else came after them.

In the car, once they were on their way, Sal said quietly to Bobby, "What happened back there? Don't think I didn't notice."

Bobby sank in his seat. He hated failing Sal. "Never been much of a fighter."

"Not what I meant." With his thumb Sal plunged in the dash lighter for the cigarette now bobbing between his lips. "I saw how scared you were. But you didn't embarrass yourself. Or me. I appreciate that."

Back at the club, Sal told Bobby and Gap to follow him into the office. "Close the door." He poured each of them a few fingers of Cutty, took a long sip of his own. "Draws a gun, the fat cunt. I'd call that a final god damn straw, how about you?" Before either of them could answer, he added, "Either of you guys like to buy in to a new room?"

THE MAN IN THE SKI MASK and baggy brown suit remained motionless in the doorway to Sal's office, gun trained straight at Bobby's face.

"Gap, Gap, put it down, okay? No need for that." Bobby stared up from where he knelt on the floor, hands held out to either side. "Think I wouldn't know it was you? I mean, I'm sorry, but hey."

The pistol sank in almost imperceptible degrees. With his free hand, the gunman reached up, pulled the ski mask off. Strands of his curly blond hair hovered from the static. Eyes whirling, he seemed wildly confused. He didn't look so much like a Hollywood type right then.

"You know what he was gonna do, right?"

"Gap, what? Sal, he—"

"No, Bobby. Listen to me. Place in Burlingame he talked about? He's got no lease. Management company's never heard of him."

"But the points, Gap, I know guys, ten, maybe a dozen, they put—"

"Shut up! Listen to me. It's bullshit. There are no points. He was just gonna close up tonight, run with the cash."

Bobby got up from the floor, using Sal's desk to pull himself onto his feet. His head spun. "Sal wouldn't do that."

"You simple? It was done."

"I don't know, Gap. Jesus." Bobby nodded to the gun. "You mind putting that thing away?"

Gap let the pistol hang beside his leg but didn't slip it in his pocket. "What was I supposed to do, Bobby? He had a gun, too."

Bobby moved toward the door. "We should check, see how bad he is."

Gap cut him off. "I'm gonna get inside the safe."

"Gap, it's Sal out there."

"I know who the fuck it is. He's a god damn thief." Sweat broke out on Gap's face. He raised the gun again, shouting now, "Okay, you got your chance. Go on home. I'm getting in that safe."

Gap waited, trying to nudge Bobby out the back way by waving the nose of the gun that direction, but Bobby couldn't move. Giving up, Gap dropped down behind Sal's desk and knelt before the vault. Bobby considered going out, checking on Sal, but as Gap worked the tumblers it dawned on him: Since when has he been planning this? More to the point, why'd he never tell me?

"I got eighteen thousand in there, Gap. My money, okay?" He eased around the corner of the desk. "I mean, I can't afford to lose my bank. Trink, she's real sick, I can't—"

Gap said nothing, just kept spinning the dial back and forth. Bobby, watching, got it then. Gap had no clue what the combination was.

"Gap, what's going on here? What's this about?"

He stood too close to ask a question like that. Sure enough, Gap spun around and the gun came with him. Bobby spooked, trying to swat the barrel away but his hand sailed high. Gap took it for a blow and on instinct fired. The bullet ripped into Bobby's arm. Maybe a second passed, maybe a thousandth of second, but Bobby stared at the small black hole torn into the fabric of his jacket, a little above the elbow. He felt the first pop of blood. And then, at last, the pain. His whole arm erupted like it had been set on fire. He cringed, winced, danced this way and that, biting his lip with all his might to keep from screaming.

"What the hell you do that for?" Both of them, same words, same time, shouted over one another.

The next thing Bobby knew he was running, out the back door Sal had told him to take in the first place. He couldn't tell if Gap was right behind, didn't dare look. He threw the lock on the door, pushed with his shoulder and tumbled out into the parking lot.

The leaves of the eucalyptus trees shivered in a brisk wind, driven by an incoming storm. Bobby's cheeks grew wet from tears as he ran to Eddie's Bug, fumbled left-handed into his right coat pocket, digging for the keys. Gap would be there any second to finish him off and Bobby wondered at what was taking him but then he was behind the wheel, cranking the ignition and lodging the tranny left-handed, fishtailing away toward the freeway.

His vision blurred as he sped north. Not just the tears. The blood loss, he was going into shock, feeling the cold possess his hands, his feet. Bullet must've hit an artery, he thought. Get yourself to a hospital. But Gap would come hunting for him, wouldn't he? To finish things. Sooner or later, probably sooner, he'd show up at the apartment. Trink was there alone.

He had to fight to keep from weaving lane to lane as he passed Candlestick Point, accelerated to clear the hill then descended past Bay View, Portola, Silver Terrace. You should call 911, he thought, tell them about Sal. But he didn't dare stop and with his arm hurt so bad he couldn't dig into his pocket for his cell phone and try to drive at the same time. "I'm sorry, Sal," he whispered. The pain spread from his arm into his shoulder, his chest, his throat. He wet himself, feeling scared like he'd never felt scared before and thinking of Eddie's mother, the smell in that house, wondering which had come first, death or the letting go.

He didn't even remember the rest of the drive or where he parked, just found himself trying to climb the seven impossible flights of stairs to the apartment. Dragging himself up along the handrail, his mind in a fog, he paused for breath at each landing with his bloody arm hanging there. The pain was everywhere now, not just his arm. He stank and had to fight from hurling but he made it to the sixth floor, stiffened his resolve and reached the next landing, halfway up.

Wait now, he thought. Maybe she's already used up the last of the Albuterol. Remember, stress is a trigger. Imagine how you look. You just tumble in like this, she'll have an attack. Too many problems at once. Too many patients. Think it through.

He knelt, hoping for just a moment to clear his head. Twisting himself into a seated position, he panted, dry-mouthed, drenched in sweat with blood caked down his sleeve, fingers sticky with it. Beneath the gore, the skin had turned a yellowish gray. Phantom shadows darted along the edges of his field of vision and to escape them he closed his eyes.

From above, he heard a door lock click. Eyes blinking open, he saw Trink staring down at him, still dressed in her underwear but she'd pulled on one of Bobby's button-down shirts as a wrap. A lit cigarette dangled between her fingers. Sneaking a midnight smoke while she waited for him to come home. Bad timing, Bobby thought.

"Roper?"

Before he could get a word out her chest started heaving. Her mouth shot open but no sound came. She dropped the cigarette and reached out blindly for the railing, finding it finally, gripping it with both hands, standing as long as she could but then her knees gave way with an awkward rubbery trembling. The whole time her eyes stayed fixed on his, staring down at him like he'd turned into something terrible.

"Baby, you gotta try," he said, loud as he could without drawing out the neighbors, his throat parched. "You gotta get up, Trink. You gotta turn around now, go back in, get your inhaler. Or if that's all used up, make coffee. Right? A couple aspirin, strong black coffee. You know what to do. Listen. We gotta get out of here. You gotta get me to a hospital, okay? Your turn to take care of me, how about that? Get up now. Come on, Trink. Try."

He might as well have said nothing. Her eyes turned vacant and she dropped sideways onto the landing, not all at once but in jerky helpless staggers as her skin turned a marbled blue. Bobby couldn't get to her, couldn't move—bad idea, he realized too late, sitting down, as much blood as you've lost. In his impotence he felt everything give—his vision grayed, his muscles went slack, his pores opened up and a bitter-smelling sweat beaded on his skin as he whispered, "Trink, please, I am so sorry." She lay on her side, eyes rolled back, mouth slack. *I'd love not to have to think about my next breath.* He closed his eyes as a sickening dizziness swept through him, like he was spinning across a dance floor, his reflection flickering beneath him.

GAP PULLED THE CAR UP as close as he could. A crowd had formed outside the apartment building. "Jesus." He turned on the wipers, to clear the windshield of spattered rain. "This is too nuts, we gotta book. Now."

Sal, sitting beside him, said nothing, just looked out at the crowd. "I'm gonna go see." He reached for the door handle but Gap reached across, grabbed his sleeve.

"You crazy? We can't stay—"

"Let go of me."

Gap didn't need to be told twice. Sal opened the door and stepped out into the street.

Gap called after him, "I'm not waiting around forever. I see anything go bad, you get into it with a cop—"

Sal cut him off. "You'll what—tell your mother?"

Sal kept hidden the fact that Gap was his stepson. It was nobody's business and you give people something to get all busy about, they'll do just that. Besides, Sal and Vivian hadn't spoken in years and what connection he had with her son he'd forged on his own—most of it, strangely, after the divorce. Sal had that kind of effect on younger men. They liked getting near him, like it was a way to prove themselves.

"I need to know where things sit." Sal closed the car door behind him and sauntered through the light rain toward the edge of the crowd.

There were too many patrol cars in the street to mean anything but a dead body. He didn't spot the morgue wagon till after. The paramedics, apparently, had already come and gone.

How did such an easy little plan go so bad, he wondered. Gather the cash, fake a stick-up, flash a gun, watch Bobby run scared—what could be simpler? That night at the Eight Ball when Phil had waved his silly little pistol around, Bobby had turned bone white, nearly crapped his pants. But tonight Bobby had hung tough, the sorry little imbecile, all for that skinny, homely freak of a chip girl—what was her name, Treblinka? That's love for you, Sal thought. It blinds you. It kills you. And then everybody left behind stands around like they haven't got a clue how a thing like this could happen but feeling secretly fascinated, even a little jealous.

He and Gap had the other marks roped in already, three hundred grand. The only one left had been Bobby and he was last because they'd fought about it. It was too easy, Sal said, taking Bobby's money but it wasn't just that. It was the way Bobby looked up to him. Sal had no problem milking suckers, it was why they existed. But Gap had pushed: They'd need every dime in Belize. The casinos were opening there, moving south from Cancun. Get positioned now, it'll be like Cuba before Castro. And Bobby won't suffer too long or hard, don't waste tears on him. He was young enough, smart enough, to start over, which wasn't true for Sal.

The weariness in his body turned leaden as he watched the coroner's staff wheel out a gurney with a body bag. He couldn't take his eyes off it.

"What happened?" Sal directed the question to a woman on the edge of the crowd. She was in her thirties—buckteeth, freckles, short hair—wearing a drab robe over sweats. She studied him a moment. Sal wondered what he must look like. His white hair sagged down onto his ears with the rain.

"This couple on the seventh floor," she said finally.

Both of them, Sal thought. The girl, too. God help me. "You live here?" It came out strangely needy.

"Yeah," she answered. Wary.

"And you know them?"

"Not much." She shrugged. "A little." She bit her lip, tucked a strand of hair behind her ear. "I thought they were carnies or something, the way the girl was tattooed. And stupid? But weird, too. I mean, she'd walk around practically naked. And the guy was, like, hypnotized."

She just kept talking after that, like he'd tripped a valve: a busybody litany of brief, edgy encounters in the lobby, the laundry room, on the stairs, described as though in some odd, misbegotten way, Bobby and the girl had deserved to die. Even as Sal told himself he should go—there was nothing this woman had to say he needed to hear—he couldn't tear himself away. Glancing back at the car he saw Gap gesturing: Hurry up. Come on. Let's go. But the woman's voice, the continuous stream of her unkind words, seemed oddly reassuring. Hypnotized, he thought. Yeah. Exactly. Something like this was bound to happen sooner or later. To them. He turned back toward the woman and started nodding along, wanting nothing so much as for her to keep talking.

Dead by Christmas

I'LL TELL YOU WHAT ruined my marriage, and it wasn't gambling or drink or chasing skirt. Our son, Donny, was walking home from a friend's house when a LeSabre blew the stop sign, ran the poor kid down in the street and dragged him twenty yards, then fled the scene.

Seven years old, Donny was. And he fought, or his body fought, half the night, until the ER surgeon came out to talk with Barb and me with that look on his face.

All I remember of the next two weeks is I went on a mission—horning my way into the loop as every department in the valley tracked down the driver, even tagging along when the arrest came down in Apache Junction. They put two men on me, to make sure I didn't take my shot as they dragged the guy out. His name was Phil Packer, an insurance adjustor with a DWI sheet ten years long, bench warrants in four counties—he'd been hiding in his girlfriend's trailer.

After that, every time Packer shuffled into court from lockup for a hearing, I was right there, front row, eye-fucking him and his wash'n'wear lawyer. None of which made a difference, of course, nor was it anything close to what Barb or our baby girl needed from me. That wasn't part of the mission.

My wife called me out on all that one night—it was late, she'd had a few, her face streaked with mascara from sitting in the dark with a bottomless cocktail and her son's ghost. Melodie, the baby, lay asleep in her room. I'd been out in the car, driving around, something I did a lot.

Seeing me there, Barb stood up and tottered closer, into the light. Her eyes were puffy and raw.

"I'm sorry. Do I know you?" She had that tone.

I said, "I had to finish up some work."

"No. I called. You left hours ago."

I had a lie ready. "A CI called, he wanted to meet. They didn't tell you?"

She laughed acidly, inches from my face now. "You're such a coward."

Looking back, I think of the things I might've done, might've said, but all I could come up with in the moment was, "How many have you had?"

"Not nearly enough." She shoved the glass into my hand, a dare. "You know, Nick, disappearing isn't the same as dying."

I remember feeling cold all over. "You're not talking sense."

"You're jealous of Donny." Her eyes, glistening in the light, turned hard. "Somehow you think staying away is going to make me miss you. The way I miss him. Christ. Are you honestly that pathetic?"

Some scientist should measure the speed at which shame turns into hate. I'll never forget that sound, never forget the feel of the glass shattering in my hand or the sight of her crumbling in front of me, no matter how much I try. There's some things "sorry" won't cure, no matter how many times you say the word, or even how much you mean it.

It's said that only one in five marriages survives the death of a child, and maybe I should take comfort in the numbers. Regardless, it was my divorce that turned me into a workhorse, not the other way around.

THIS WAS THE EARLY nineties and I'd rotated in to robbery, great place to get lost, the numbing paperwork, sixteen hour days if you want them. There were four of us from different departments—Phoenix, Tempe, Scottsdale, Mesa—meeting once a week to share intel. We'd had twenty restaurant take-downs around the valley the previous six months, all the same guy. He came in at closing, when the back door was propped open by the kitchen crew—that's when they dragged the rubber mats out to the parking lot for the nightly hose-down. Meanwhile, inside, the money was getting counted and bagged for deposit.

The robber wore dark coveralls, gloves, a ski mask, and he always slipped in and out within minutes, which meant he knew the business. Brandishing a snubnose, he'd prone out the manager, tie him up with plastic cuffs, the kind they use for riot control, then snatch the night deposit. Right before leaving, he'd grab the manager's wallet, dig out the driver's license. "You're gonna say some wetback did this," he'd whisper. "I know your name. I know where you live." Even after we found out the guy was white, we still had vics swearing to our faces he was Mexican.

Finally, luck stepped in, as it does more times than most cops care to admit.

Two cars responded to a domestic here in Tempe—how's that for poetic? One cop grabbed the husband, the other took the wife, separated them, different rooms. The wife—eye swollen shut, cracked lip—she bawls to the cop there with her, "You know all the restaurant jobs around here the past few months? That asshole in the next room, he's the one you're after."

The woman wouldn't swear out a statement, though, so the uniform tracks me down in robbery at the end of his shift, to give me a verbal. I'm Tempe's case agent on the restaurant spree. You can imagine, he lays out the scenario, I'm cringing a little. Some guy tuning up his wife. Everybody on the force knew my business. Even so, I should've been thrilled, right? Finally, a suspect.

The guy was Mike Gallardi, his wife's name was Rhonda. Together, they ran a hole-in-the-wall called Mike's Place out on Baseline Road in South Phoenix. You could get a coronary just reading the menu but the place was clean, with a small counter and maybe a half dozen booths.

Here's the thing: They catered to cops. You walked in, one whole wall was dedicated to fallen officers. Flash a badge, your kids got free sodas with their meals. Come in on duty and no one's around? Boom, wink, you ate free.

I'd been at their place just once, a couple years before, taken there by a buddy of mine in Traffic Division. Rhonda worked the register and counter, a shy, chesty, bleached-out woman in her thirties. Mike was the talker and he came out from behind the grill to toady up, all shucks and gee-whiz.

How to say this—I don't trust people who backslap cops. They always want something. Not that I made much headway on that point when I broke my news to the robbery roundtable.

"No way Mike's the suspect." This from Cavanaugh, the detective from Phoenix. "I can name fifty guys right now, this minute, who'll vouch for him."

"His own old lady handed him up."

"After he batted her around, yeah. Go back, now that she's cooled off. I'll bet she admits it's crap."

He had a point, of course, domestics being what they are. But something about the way he said it clued me in to what he really meant: *What would your wife spill about you, Boghossian, if we gave her half a chance?*

THANKFULLY, THE FOUR COMMANDERS overseeing the roundtable agreed with me and ordered surveillance. The teams worked in rotation, each department on for three days then making way for the next detail. But Mike was smart. He made our guys early and burned them in heat runs, crazy Ivans, every kind of stunt you can imagine to flush them out. Once he just stopped in traffic, walked back to the unmarked car and said, "Why are you following me? I haven't done anything."

I could just picture him, over one of those free burgers or shrimp baskets he doled out, pumping guys for information on tail jobs: C'mon, tell me, I'm just so doggone curious. And cops—hated by damn near everybody, grateful for anyone who gives a rat's ass—they couldn't tell him their stories fast enough.

It got to me, sure. We were the ones who'd trained this guy—inadvertently, granted, but he was smarter than he should've been because of us. He was pulling out our wallets, whispering our names and addresses. And yeah, like everybody else he'd chumped, I felt ashamed.

Meanwhile, Mike adapted, lying low for a month, wise to how we'd think. And sure enough, the surveillance sergeants pulled the plug, they needed the bodies. Not a week later, Mike hit his next restaurant, and this time he upped the ante.

It happened out in Mesa. The manager saw Mike coming, locked himself in the office, dialed 911. Mike fired through the door—his first use of actual violence, not just threats. The manager, terrified, let him in.

Mike went for the man's ID first thing, recited the usual, then dug further through his wallet and found pictures. "Two little girls. You love 'em?" The rest went fast, Mike barking orders. He was long gone before the responding units arrived. And the manager, he wouldn't say word one till his wife confirmed by phone there was a squad car stationed outside their house. The next day, no notice, he moved his whole family to Denver. Even left the furniture behind.

"I STILL DON'T BUY Mike's our man," Cavanaugh said at our next get-together. "But I agree renewing surveillance makes sense—nab him or move on, quicker the better."

The commanders chimed in, each department adding bodies, with new directions to lie back. They were sick of taking the burns.

Two weeks later, I got a call from surveillance. "Boghossian, get this. Gallardi and his wife locked up their place as usual but didn't head home. They checked into a hotel on the frontage road along I-10."

I knew the strip, we all did: a line of restaurants flanked that part of the freeway.

As I drove on over I thought about Rhonda's tagging along. It surprised me, I'll be honest. Maybe Cavanaugh had been right—I should've gone up to her early, asked her to confirm what she'd said that night Mike trashed her. And even though I knew that would've tipped our hand, now she wasn't just keeping mum, she was joining in. I felt responsible, like there'd been a point in time when I could have saved her. No surprise, I felt like that a lot back then.

I met the team at the hotel and, sure enough, after eleven, Mike came out of the room in dark coveralls, a day pack around his waist. He walked down a side street to the parking lot of an Applebee's, then hunkered down in a patch of oleander to watch the kitchen crew do its thing. The radios started to buzz—we had our man, no more doubts. After a half hour, Mike eased out of the bushes, retraced his steps and slipped back into his and Rhonda's hotel room.

THE NEXT DAY, when I called the robbery roundtable together to report, Cavanaugh went from looking like he'd lost his dog to acting like he meant to kill somebody.

"Okay," he said finally, "I'm in. If Mike Gallardi's our guy he'll get no favors from me."

I volunteered for surveillance at Applebee's, even though it meant staying alert for hours on end with the windows rolled up in hundred degree heat, drinking warm Coke and pissing it all back into the empty cup.

At nine, our eyes at Mike's Place reported that Rhonda had left, heading toward home. An hour later, Mike locked up and followed suit. A collective moan went out over the radio. He'd called it off. Then, not long after, we heard that Mike and Rhonda were on the move again, leaving the house together. They were on their way toward us.

The voices on the radio perked back up—this was the night, we could feel it. And we knew we'd have to watch the whole thing play out, let him go in, rob the place, or it'd come apart in court. But what if he sniffed us out? What if he took a hostage?

Rhonda drove down one of the side streets and parked, then Mike hopped out, headed for the parking lot. I slouched in my seat, a drunk snoring off a bender. Through slit eyelids I watched him saunter toward the back of Applebee's, and for an instant he looked straight at me. It was dark, some serious distance separated us. Even so, I sat stock still, wondering if I'd been made.

He turned away and ducked inside the concrete dumpster enclosure. Two other men with eyes on the door reported they had visual, and we had a man out front, too, in case Mike tried to run that way. Surveillance units got in position to take down Rhonda when the time came.

At half past eleven, the kitchen crew trooped out, propped the back door open and dragged out their slimy black mats, sudsing them up, hosing them down. I kept up my ruse, dripping with sweat but not moving, sipping air through the window crack. Mike stayed put, too, even after the kitchen crew vanished again, leaving the door open as they mopped the floors. After midnight they humped on out again, collected their mats and dragged them back inside.

A whisper crackled on the radio, "What's he waiting for?" Another whisper snapped back, "Off the air." We were all raw from the heat, testy from sitting still so long. Over the next hour, the employees came out in ones or twos, lingering for a smoke before driving away. Finally, the manager trudged out, locked up, not carrying a deposit bag—he'd left it in the safe—then got in his car and left.

Mike waited another fifteen minutes before sliding out of the dumpster enclosure. Hands in his pockets, he meandered across the parking lot, shooting one last glance my direction. Minutes later, surveillance confirmed that he and Rhonda were headed back home.

We waited in place another two hours. Mike might come back, I thought, try to burglarize the place, clip the trunk line on the alarm, pop the safe. Finally, I called in to Rooney, the grave-yard sergeant, to report. "I want everybody to stay put, Roon. The money's all there, he's coming back in the morning when they open up."

"I'm calling it off," Rooney said. "Your guys have been stuck in their cars for six hours. It's still what, ninety-five degrees out-side? Besides, from the sound of it, you got made."

"The sound of what? You're not sitting here."

"I need a team to report to the rail yards. Call just came in. Somebody made off with two dozen cases of Heineken."

I almost spit. "You're pulling my guys off because a pack of kids rifled a boxcar?"

"We've got a squeaky victim."

"Meaning who?"

"Meaning the Westbrook family."

The Westbrooks, wholesale distributors throughout the state, in-laws at the statehouse, a cousin in Congress. Somebody asks you what it's like to be a cop, I thought, tell them this story.

I got home to my apartment about three, showered the sticky grit off my skin and crawled into bed. I still wasn't used to sleeping by myself back then and I lay awake awhile, puzzling the whole thing through. Get a cop alone, find him on a day he wants to be honest, he'll tell you the cases that bothered him most always involved a suspect who someway, somehow, reminded him of himself. And I knew Mike Gallardi pretty well, I thought. Down deep, where it mattered, he was weak. That's why he liked power, not just over Rhonda but the people he robbed—gunpoint, the terror in their eyes. *Do what I tell you.* Like a cop, or his bent idea of one: a guy who gets what he wants, even hammers his wife, and never pays. I was going to change that. I'd be the one who finally made sure he suffered, if only for the chance to tell myself I was different. I was better.

Eventually, I drifted off and dreamed I stood in the doorway of a house off in the desert somewhere. A wounded dog limped toward me through the moonlit chaparral. As it drew close, I looked into its eyes, and saw my son looking back at me.

The next thing, the phone was ringing.

It was Rooney. "I don't know what to say, Nick. Appelbee's got hit this morning, eight o'clock." Some throat-clearing. "Just like you said."

I rubbed my face, checked my watch. Eight-thirty. "How much?"

"Twelve grand."

Hardly a take worth risking your freedom for, I thought. But this wasn't just about money. I wondered if Mike had driven back alone, or if he'd dragged Rhonda along with him again.

And maybe she didn't feel bullied at all. Maybe, for the first time in a long, long while, she felt married.

"WE'RE NEVER GONNA CATCH this guy without a wire." I was laying out my case to John Tally, the county attorney. "He's getting cocky, cocky crooks get sloppy and that's when people get hurt."

Tally tented his hands, rocking in his chair, sunlight flaring in the windows behind him. An ASU man, politician to the bone, he was tan and fit, pompous, cutthroat. "I'll approve a wire," he said finally. "And a task force, but I want hard numbers on bodies."

"Phoenix and Tempe'll pony up ten men apiece," I said, guessing. "Scottsdale and Mesa half that each, an even thirty."

"You're lead agent," he said pointedly. "Team up with Tom Kolchek for the wire affidavit. And don't be fooled by his looks. He's the smartest guy I've got."

I stood up to leave. "I want to call off the surveillance, make the target think he's in the clear."

Tally glanced up, like I'd already become a bother. "I told you," he said. "You're lead agent."

TALLY WAS RIGHT, Kolchek looked like your Uncle Monty—thick all over with thinning hair and sad-sack eyes—but he was one of the sharpest cops I ever worked with. The affidavit came to a hundred pages and was airtight, detailing every job, how Mike came to be our suspect, the ensuing surveillance, the continuing robberies, everything. We argued that, given Rhonda's new accomplice role, phone communications between the house and the restaurant could prove fruitful. The judge granted us thirty days for the wire, with a re-up possible for another thirty if the need arose, which would carry us through the holidays. But if we didn't have results by then, tough. We'd have to bag up and go home.

We notified the phone company of our target lines and anticipated start date, so they could build the parallel circuits for the wiretap. Two days later, they called back to tell us Mike had disconnected his home phone. He'd done it the same day we submitted the affidavit.

Kolchek hung up and sat there, thinking it through. Finally, in an oddly sunny voice, he said, "We'll bug his house."

"You don't get it," I told him.

"I get it," Kolchek said. "So? We tighten the circle of who knows what, rewrite the affidavit, wire up his house. Maybe we'll get lucky. You get any better ideas, let me know."

I didn't get any better ideas, of course. And every time I tried to imagine who might be tipping Mike off, I could never convince myself I had the right man. Cavanaugh was the first and obvious choice, given how long he'd stuck up for Mike, but he was a hard cop and I'd seen the betrayal in his face before the Applebee's job. Besides, like he'd said, fifty cops would vouch for Mike in a heartbeat—any one of them could be our leak.

Kolchek and I reworked the affidavit, kept the wire on the restaurant phone and asked for three transmitters for the residence—one in the living room, one in the dining room, one in the bedroom—sensitive enough, at ten thousand dollars a pop, to catch voices throughout the house. The judge signed off and Kolchek introduced me to a tech for the county attorney's office named Pritchard, who'd go in and actually set things up.

"I'll go with," I told Kolchek.

"No, I will," he said. "I'm a pretty good lock pick and we only need two men inside."

"What about the dog?"

Kolchek cocked his head. "Dog?"

"A white shepherd," I said. "It's in the surveillance reports."

"Right. I remember. What's your point?"

"I used to work canine. The white ones are unpredictable, you don't want to go in there alone." That was mostly crap, but there was no way I wasn't going with them. I wanted a look inside that house.

The next day, when Mike and Rhonda were at the restaurant, Kolchek walked up their front walk and took a Polaroid, then went to the hardware store, bought an identical door and set it up in his office, practicing till it took only forty-five seconds to pop both locks.

Meanwhile, I scoped the neighborhood for the best spot to place the undercover van. Mike and Rhonda lived in a maze-like community of townhouses grouped in quads, and the geometry of the place was all wrong; there was no place within a hundred yards of their unit to park the van and not stand out. Then I saw there was a unit for rent one quad over. We could set up the wire room in there, as long as we kept a low profile.

I hit up Tally's office for the rent and two days later, when Mike and Rhonda and most of the neighbors were off to work, we moved our guys in. Me, Kolchek and Pritchard headed over for our entry to plant the bugs, while a ram car took up position on the street in case Mike or Rhonda came back while we were still inside the house.

When we got to the front porch, though, we found a brand new security gate with two additional locks, barring access to the door. Kolchek just stood there, staring, holding his lockpick tools. "This isn't happening." He glanced at his watch and swallowed hard. Inside, the dog was barking like the place was on fire.

I started heading for the back of the house. "Bet you're glad you brought me along now."

There was a privacy wall around the patio in back and I scaled it, dropping down onto the pavers. A sliding Arcadia door led inside, with an insert for a doggy door. I got down on the ground, reached through and flicked aside the dowel lodging the door in place. The dog realized what was happening then, and as I slipped inside he turned a corner and charged toward me, hackling up, fangs bared.

I reached frantically in my pocket for the syringe of Isoforine I'd brought along to knock him out, only to sink my thumb into the needle. I played air banjo with my hand for a second, saying something original like, "Goddamnmother*fuck*," then glanced up and saw I wasn't the only one to miscalculate. As his paws hit linoleum, the dog lost traction, sliding toward me helplessly. Stepping forward, I caught him under the jaw with a kick so fierce he cartwheeled backwards.

"Get in the god damn bathroom!"

The dog sulked off, mewling, as I checked my thumb, hoping adrenalin would ward off any grogginess. Suddenly, I remembered my dream from weeks before—the lonely house, the wounded dog. A chirp from my radio broke the spell.

I clicked on. "Yeah?"

"We heard that, detective." It was one of my guys in the wire room. In the background, laughter. "Punt the pooch—that what they teach you in canine?"

I switched off my radio and searched out the front door. When I got there I found out the security gate was locked from inside, requiring a key. "This nails it," I told Kolchek through the grating. "Somebody's tipping this guy off."

"We'll talk about it later," Kolchek whispered, standing exposed with Pritchard on the porch. "Get us inside."

Kolchek lacked the physique to scale the privacy wall, so I found a window in a small utility room near the back for the two men to crawl through. Once everybody was inside, we headed to the living room to set up shop. Kolchek got busy taking Polaroids of the room so we could put it back the same way we found it.

"Look at this," I said, pointing to the couch. There were sheets, blankets, a pillow. "Christ, she's kicked him out of bed. They're in the middle of another fight."

"Get to work," Kolchek said. He was testy and pouring sweat. It dawned on me then that, despite a first-rate mind, Kolchek lacked any serious operational experience. The glitch with the locks had rattled him.

Pritchard hooked up his transmitters to the phone lines. Even though the service had been cut off, the wires still held voltage. We set them up in the three different rooms as planned, and Pritchard asked me to contact the wire room to see if we were live. Only then did I realize I hadn't switched my radio back on after that crack about my canine prowess. When I flipped the button, a voice came through almost screaming. "Jesus, Boghossian, where'd you go? We've been trying to contact you for ten minutes. The wife's on her way, just west of Pepperwood. You're lucky she stopped for smokes. Move!"

We rushed to test the transmitters through the wire room and got an all-clear. Kolchek's hands shook so bad from nerves he couldn't screw the plates back on the phone plugs, so I took the screwdriver from him, told him to pack up with Pritchard, I'd close up.

They scrambled out the utility room window and I locked it behind them. Turning back to finish up, something caught my eye, something I'd overlooked before.

On a shelf near the door, a small day pack rested among some other odds and ends.

We had no warrant to search the house or its contents, but I took the day pack down regardless and opened it up: A ski mask. A pair of black garden gloves. A .38 snubnose and a dozen plastic cuffs.

There was a desk in the room and I laid the contents out, retrieved the Polaroid from the dining room and took a picture. This was a trophy, not evidence—I wouldn't even tell anybody about it, let alone show them the picture. The whole investigation might vanish down a hole if guys started jabbering. I packed everything up again and put the day pack back where I'd found it, but then my curiosity got the best of me and I searched the desk. In the bottommost drawer, I found a snapshot—Mike with Cavanaugh, up in the mountains somewhere. They were hunting together, carrying shotguns, the best of friends from their smiles. Rhonda, I guess, had snapped the picture. I took another Polaroid. This too, of course, wasn't evidence, and I told myself it didn't really prove anything. It was just a reminder— my reminder—of what I might be up against.

I ran back to the dining room and was just about finished putting things back in place when the voice came through my radio again: "Boghossian, she's at the corner."

I barked into the mouthpiece, "Ram her!"

I was making one last check, comparing where everything was with the Polaroids, when I heard the collision outside. It was about fifty yards from the house, some undercover cop plowing into Rhonda's back end at the stop sign. I opened the bathroom door and told the dog to stay, then headed toward the patio, fit the doggy door insert into place and reached through and slipped the dowel back onto the runner.

Through the glass of the sliding door, I saw the large white dog slink into view. Our eyes met. He flinched a little, tail lodged between his legs. Ashamed, like everybody else.

IT WAS UP TO THE BOYS in the wire room now. I checked in as often as I could, but the days went by, nothing. Mike knew we'd been in there—tipped off by Cavanaugh, I supposed, something I had to keep to myself. Besides which, just like I'd thought, Mike and Rhonda were in a tiff, the two of them seldom speaking.

As time passed, though, I felt strangely encouraged. I knew the dynamics of the simmering fight. I heard the cues—the caustic one-liners, the icy silences. Somehow, some night, something would set them off. And the words would come boiling out, things they'd regret forever.

As it turned out, that night came right before Thanksgiving. And the somehow and something of it proved, to my way of thinking anyway, too apropos.

The surveillance team trailed Mike to a porno arcade near the airport. We'd watched him visit smut shops and strip clubs all over the valley, not sure if he was casing the places or had just grown tired of not getting any at home. This time, though, according to the cop watching from the parking lot, Mike came out wobbly.

"I may be wrong," the radio voice reported, "but I think our boy just had himself a little love."

When Mike got home he wasn't inside five minutes before he launched into Rhonda—a fight over nothing, but so blistering everybody in the wire room shuddered. When one of the cops reached out to turn off the recorder, though, honoring the minimization guidelines, I told him, "Wait." We'd gotten our first lead in this case after a brawl between these two. I could justify listening on the grounds there was a reasonable expectation that, in their fury, one of them would say something useful. Accusing.

The voices kept rising, more and more shrill and cruel. And sexual. One Mormon on the wire crew blushed, but everybody kept listening, each of us wondering what we should do if, at some point, one of them tried to kill the other. And yes, finally, we heard scuffling. I reached for the phone to dial dispatch as I heard Rhonda stammer oddly, "M-Mike, n-no. No!" The yelling turned to muffled cries, then rhythmic, whimpering moans. Gradually it dawned on us that Mike had decided on a little show'n'tell, to demonstrate for Rhonda what had happened earlier that night, during his encounter at the porn hole.

"One good pipe cleaning deserves another," somebody cracked.

"Turn off the machine," I said, knowing we'd get nothing of any use now. Adding insult to injury, Mike moved back into the bedroom that night. So that's how you make your marriage work, I thought, hating him even more.

THE FIRST THIRTY DAYS played out, no results. We got an extension but none of the departments would pony up the manpower like before. They put rookies on the line-of-sight details.

Once, after letting one tail car pass him, Mike chased the cop all the way down Central Avenue, flashing his brights, just to embarrass the kid.

Meanwhile the wire crew was going batty listening to nothing and more of nothing. We were back where we'd started—we'd never catch Mike Gallardi except red-handed, coming out the back of a restaurant. And everything we knew about him said, if that happened, he'd make us kill him.

"The man's gonna be dead by Christmas," someone quipped, and it became the unofficial slogan of the whole operation, until I told everybody to knock it off. "If you're right, and we take him out, you don't want to have to explain that little mantra to Internal Affairs."

Given where we stood, though, I decided it was time to tickle the wire. I went to Tally again, told him we needed to put some pressure on the couple, inflict a little fear.

I SHOWED UP AT Rhonda's front door when surveillance confirmed Mike was at the restaurant alone. I came in a marked unit, the strobe spinning out at the curb, and the uniform who'd driven stood with me on the porch. No more avoiding the neighbors—we wanted their attention now. Inside, the dog went off when the doorbell rang, then went still, dropping his tail, when he saw me beyond the grating.

Rhonda deadpanned, "Gee, if I didn't know better, I'd think you and the dog knew each other."

I pulled the subpoena from my jacket pocket and gestured for her to open the security gate. "Rhonda Gallardi, you're to appear before the grand jury on December 5th. You're not to discuss your scheduled appearance or the subject matter of your testimony with anyone except your lawyer—not even your husband. Understood?"

She looked taken aback but hardly stunned—some fright in her eyes, but a baiting grin too. I wondered if that was how she looked right before Mike hit her.

"What if I don't open the door?"

"I'll just set it down on the porch here. Either way, you're served."

The grin faded a bit, her fear quickening into anger as her eyes checked the cop behind me, then slid back. "This is harassment."

"Guess how many times a day I hear that."

"Because you're a prick?"

I nodded for the cop to head back to the car. Once he was out of earshot, I said, "Know what I think? You've been trying hard for a long time to make things work—your restaurant, your marriage. I admire that. But the point where things were gonna change is gone for good." I stuck my hands in my pockets, to look harmless. "You want to turn that around, now's the time."

Women who've been hit more than once have a look—sad and yet defiant, almost mocking, but defeated all the same. Come on, I thought, invite me in, talk to me. I knew, given the chance, I could open her up, end this thing. But her eyes turned hard and far-away again. "Leave your papers on the porch," she said, then shut the door.

IN THE WIRE ROOM, we listened when Mike came home that night. Apparently, what I'd said registered, at least a little, because the good wife unloaded.

"No more! I'm done."

"Shut up, Rhonda."

"I'm not gonna lie under oath for you! I never wanted—"

"I said shut the fuck up, Rhonda!"

The sound of scuffling came again. I grabbed the phone to dial dispatch. But a minute later, they were outside the house, walking the dog. The perfect couple—Mike with his arm around Rhonda's shoulder, holding her close, loving, protective, whispering into her hair.

RHONDA GOT COACHED WELL for her grand jury appearance. All her answers reduced to: I don't remember. I'm not sure. I don't think so. I don't know.

"He beat us," I told my guys afterward, like I was confessing to some crime of my own.

A week later we went in to pull the wires, and I was hardly shocked to see they'd put a three-piece console in front of the wall socket where we'd planted the living room transmitter. They'd been a step ahead of us the whole time. Took us an hour, though, to take the knickknacks down, drag the big thing away, claim our bug then push the monster back and make sure all the junk was in the right place again, even smoothing the carpet so you couldn't tell anything had moved.

The operation got bagged, departments couldn't justify the manpower any more. We went around to restaurants, schooling them on smarter ways to close up at night—it was all we could do at that point. Maybe Mike would decide his luck had played out. Or maybe he'd get reckless, hurt somebody, and the whole thing would heat up all over again.

* * *

ON CHRISTMAS EVE, I visited Barb and our daughter for the annual holiday torture—unwanted presents, forced smiles. And no talk of Donny, as though the only thing that could keep the pain at bay was a punishing silence.

Walking to my car, though, I heard the front door click open behind me. Turning, I saw my daughter—she was five then—running toward me in her red velvet dress and green tights. Behind her, Barb waited in the doorway, a silhouette.

Melodie scooted up, gripped my hand and pulled so I'd bend down. In a solemn whisper, she said, "Don't be sad, okay? It's Christmas."

"I'm not sad," I lied, but she'd already dropped my hand, spun around and fled back toward her mother who let her back in, then closed the door.

Later at my own place, drinking scotch as I flipped through the channels, I got the call from dispatch. A steak house up in Paradise Valley got hit right at closing. I was on my way to the scene when the second call came in. Shots fired. The address made my stomach drop.

BY THE TIME I got to the condo the place was alive with cops, strobes spinning around the complex, mingling eerily with the Christmas lights. I got out of my car and pushed through the crowd of neighbors outside. The cop with the entry/exit log took my name and badge number, then waved me in.

Techs and detectives ambled about. A spindly tree stood in the living room, sagging with ornaments and tinsel. One of the guys from homicide pointed me back to the kitchen.

In the breakfast nook, I found a uniformed cop standing guard over Cavanaugh, who sat gripping his head. He glanced up just long enough to catch my eye, his gaze frantic with calculation.

To the uniform, I said, "Do everybody a favor and stand back a little. He makes a grab for your gun, you may both wind up dead."

From the kitchen I made way toward the utility room. A body sheet covered a sprawling form on the floor, a pool of drying blood trailing out from underneath. Spray patterns hazed the walls. An eerie hand print smeared the doorframe.

In the bedroom, wearing an undershirt and cargo shorts, Rhonda sat with hollow eyes, stroking the shepherd, who lay at her feet whimpering. A female officer stood guard, one hand on her sidearm, as though she intended to shoot the dog if it so much as moved.

It took a second for Rhonda to sense I was there in the doorway. Glancing up, she blinked, took me in. Her hair was a mess. She looked ashen and lost.

Cavanaugh would take the fall, pleading out to manslaughter. His story—I can't say whether it's true or not, though I tend to believe more than I doubt—was that he and Rhonda, his cop-crazy buddy's wife, were lovers. The night Mike found out, he knocked Rhonda around a while, then went out, got coked up and took down his first restaurant. He'd been pumping Cavanaugh for information on robberies for ages, claiming he just wanted to know how to protect his own place.

Mike came back from that first job in an odd heat, feeling invincible—the man he was meant to be—and told Rhonda that, if he ever went down, he'd hand up her lover as the man who'd taught him everything. Cavanaugh had to protect him then, to protect himself, protect Rhonda. He began tipping Mike off on the robbery investigations, staying away from Rhonda once the surveillance began but getting messages through by using the guy who washed dishes at their restaurant as a go-between. That went on until Rhonda's grand jury appearance, after which she told Mike she'd dime him out herself if he didn't stop, she didn't care who got hurt. And Mike obliged her—until Christmas Eve.

He missed it, that nervy heat when he slipped in, pointing the gun. The fear. The begging.

As soon as he left the house for Paradise Valley, Rhonda picked up the phone, dialed Cavanaugh, told him she was leaving for good, she'd had it. He told her to wait, he'd be right over. They meant to be gone by the time Mike got back but—here again I'm not sure what to believe—he surprised them, slipping into the house unnoticed. It was self-defense, if you looked at it right, though Cavanaugh knew better than to take that to trial.

But all of that was yet in the telling as I stood there in the bedroom doorway. The dog ignored me for once, still whimpering, its ears pricked up. It was Rhonda who stared right at me.

"You're the one whose wife walked out," she said finally. She left the rest hanging, but her voice was accusing. She wouldn't be gloated over, not by the likes of me.

I don't know how to explain it. Despite her contempt, despite everything, I felt for her. And I could afford to be gracious, not because I was different or better or even because it was Christmas. I remembered my daughter's words, whispered in my ear: Don't be sad, okay? I had a piece of something back I'd thought was lost for good. It felt a little like being forgiven.

"My wife had good reason to leave," I said, thinking: Why lie?

But Rhonda just turned away. With a soft, miserable laugh, she said, "Like that's all it takes."

With profound thanks to Detective Jay Pirouznia, Tempe PD (Retired)

Killing Yourself to Survive

SATCHER IGNORED HIS CELL PHONE, preferring to watch Odilia as she groaned herself upright on the edge of the bed. Sunlight flared in the lacework curtains beside her; the drone of traffic along the Avenida la Reforma filtered in through the window. She yawned, absently finger-combing the snarls from her long black hair. The call, he knew, was from Colburn. It could wait, for now.

Up and awake for nearly half an hour, he'd long completed

his morning constitutional, even made a wretched pot of coffee in the bathroom with the hissing gurgling device the hotel provided, and now, dressed in just his briefs and a hand-embroidered *guayabera* bought at the Mercado Central, he sat tapping away on his laptop, plowing through the third wall of usernames and passwords and encryption keys to access the private sanctum of his emails. Even with Ethernet one couldn't be too careful, and only an idiot, or someone setting a trap, would rely on hotel wireless.

"I should not have drink so much," she said, voice furry from her hangover.

Satcher finally plucked his cell off the desk and shot a glance at the display—message routed through to voicemail, good. "I can muster up a second pot of coffee, if you'd like."

She seemed to draw the words in like a warning, reflect on them, only to shake her head, her backlit hair quivering down her shoulders. Feeling gentlemanly, he tried not to stare at her breasts, but it was curious how girlish she was up top, how womanly at the hips. Then again, she was nothing if not a puzzle: the long Mayan nose, the thin Castilian lips, the paleness of her skin despite its *indígena* architecture, the little thumb-hold of flesh beneath her chin, the incongruous overbite that made her smile explode.

She'd been a wallflower at the embassy gathering in her pastel suit and sling-back pumps, holding her champagne flute like a candle, a local prosecutor assisting the UN team targeting the militarized mafias roaming the country with impunity these days. It was, Satcher thought at the time, a heady job for a twenty-something whose principal claim to worldliness was a year in New Orleans studying international relations and Emily Dickinson at Loyola.

Sensing an opportunity, he'd snatched a bottle of Dom Perignon from a passing waiter and kept replenishing not just his glass but hers, flirting, flattering, chatting her up, watching her grow from shy to giggly to tipsy, at which point he stole her away to the Zona Viva for the usual playful nonsense, showing some cards, not many, the occasional necessary lie—he told her he was a risk analyst for an American investment consortium, trying to determine which opportunities in Guatemala City were little more than money-laundering fronts.

When they finally kissed, the heat rippled through him a little more than he'd expected, and he actually shivered when she reached around with her fingertips and stroked the bristle at his nape. She had that thing you look for, the strength and yet the gentleness, the old-world grace that can't be faked, the smarts, the fire, the simple decent kindness of a genuinely nice lady who, thankfully, likes to fuck.

Using her blazer for an umbrella, they'd run through a light rain to his hotel, where shyness fled and clothing flew—she straddled him, hands pumping his chest like cat's paws and the tips of her black hair grazing his face as she stumbled in and out of English with her endearments. Afterward she'd nuzzled his throat then curled beneath his arm, resting her head on his heart and tracing her fingertips across his shoulder blades, murmuring as she drifted off, "You need wake me *temprano*, okay?"

The cell phone started humming again and it seemed to snap her into gear—glancing about the bed and floor, tucking a strand of hair behind her ear, finding her blouse, slipping her arms into the gauzy sleeves as she rose and fled to the bathroom.

Satcher flipped open his phone.

"Been a bit of a cock-up, mate." As expected, Colburn. "You decent?"

A trace of Odilia's scent lingered in her wake. "Never."

"I'm serious, Satchmo. Bloody fucking mess, I'm afraid."

Satcher glanced at his watch. "When and where?"

"Lobby. Yours, not mine. Fifteen. Look smart."

Satcher snapped his phone shut as, beyond the bathroom door, Odilia flushed the john and cranked open the spigots, the water a muffled drum roll against the tile of the shower stall. He went around, gathered her things, laid them out primly on the bed, then finished dressing himself, slipped on his cargo pants, laced up his boots. He punched in the combination code on the safe in the closet, removed his holstered Sig, looped it onto his belt and fit it to the small of his back, letting the billowing fall of his *guayabera* conceal the weapon. Look smart.

Odilia's shower permitted him time for one last glance at his email, and he scrolled through the more recent intelligence updates and in-house memoranda, then changed identities, rummaged through his personal Inbox and found a message from his son, Brandon. The boy had sent along a drawing from art class, sent in the body of the transmission, not an attachment, good boy. No text with it, typical, not a verbal kid. He had a gift for pen drawings, an intense idiosyncratic style that spoke of a feverish misery; he was generally placid in temperament, withdrawn, but once a week or so something snagged an inner tripwire, detonating rages so scathing he had no friends. Even pets were out of the question. The meticulous art work seemed to calm him, or so said Julia, Satcher's ex.

What had it been, he thought, scrolling down to the picture, a year, maybe longer since he'd visited the boy. The image, as always, seemed to ripple with dread: a vast array of arrows of various shapes and styles, feathery and delicate to massive and dense black, pointing every possible direction, a compass in the mind of a god gone mad. The arrows were tucked and linked and nestled together in oddly symmetrical configurations, suggesting both an impossibly random confusion and yet a subtle radiation from an invisible core. At the bottom, written in that distinctive scrawl: *The Users and the Used.*

Specialists had probed and questioned and offered referrals, only to pencil-tap their chins or throw up their hands, not that their ignorance stopped them from plying the boy with an ever-evolving brew of pharmaceutical cocktails. Satcher couldn't keep up with the changes in regimen, not that he'd tried terribly hard.

He was logging off as Odilia reappeared, scurrying about, stepping into her panties, shimmying into her skirt, tucking in her blouse, then earrings, necklace, bracelet, shoes. Satcher considered stopping her, stealing another half hour, knowing he couldn't and feeling strangely aroused less at the chance than its impossibility. What's happened to you, he wondered, feeling the full effect of the dreariness fogging his soul and suffering a momentary impulse to tell her how stunning and smart and brave she was, how unlike anyone he'd ever met. He wanted to confide in her, blurt out *I've wasted every minute of my misbegotten life.* But he knew not to mistake romance for redemption, suspected she did too.

Gathering her purse, draping her jacket over her arm, she took one last look around, tucked her hair behind her ear again, a girlish tic, then offered one last popping smile.

He said, "Probably best I not head down with you." It came out a little more curt than he'd intended.

Her smile faltered. "No." Fussing with her jacket, her purse, she stood there awkwardly, sweetly, then stepped toward him, took his face in her hand and eased up on tiptoe to confer her goodbye kiss, lingering longer than he'd expected, and he bit back what it aroused. Finally, manners kicking in, that or good sense, he found a notepad atop the desk, a pen, scrawled his cell number. Tearing the top sheet off, he handed it to her. "I'm here for another week, I think."

"Thank you," she said, slipping the note into the pocket of her skirt, then one last over-the-shoulder smile as she left.

COLBURN SAT DEEP IN one of the lobby sofas, paging through the *International Herald Tribune* and sipping tea from a hotel mug. Glancing up as Satcher approached, he offered by way of greeting, "Nice bit of chuff flounced out just a couple ticks ago. Yours?"

"Don't be vulgar."

Colburn set his mug on a nearby tray. "I said she was nice."

The valet brought the car around, Colburn dropped behind the wheel, Satcher the opposite side. "Lope rang me up this morning," Colburn said, referring to their principal local informant. "Shot me out of a dead sleep, must've been what, quarter past six? If that. Said there was something we mustn't miss at one of the local *calequeros*."

"He's meeting us?"

"Given what I expect we'll see there, can't imagine having Lope anywhere near would be wise."

Lope, aka Ramon Parada-Lopez, was Colburn's contact in the local underworld, a slot machine for general background. Formerly a commando with the Kaibil corps, Lope had links to a kidnapping ring here in GC comprised of other skulkers from the special forces branch and a few bent cops—exactly the kind of operation, Satcher thought, that Odilia was trying to expose and prosecute. He admired that about her, and knew that what she and her colleagues hoped to accomplish was an honorable thing, in theory. It wasn't why he'd put the make on her, but it hadn't hurt either. And in the long run, their objectives coincided. But in the short run, men like Lope were indispensible. And in the grand scheme, given the impatience of powerful men, the short run always held the cards.

A light rain fell, the wipers chugged, leaving filmy threads of moisture across the windshield. Colburn leaned forward over the steering wheel, softly whistling his old regimental double-past, "The Road to the Isles," as he read street signs, weaving his way through Zona 4, past the Botanical Gardens, then merging onto 7 Avenida and passing the National Theater as they plunged straight into the heart of Zona 1.

It was home to the Metropolitan Cathedral and the Plaza Mayor, and for a moment Satcher tried to see it as Odilia might, still graced with promise, even nobility. Once beyond the historical center, though, the shops and apartments lining the street looked disconsolate, not just from the rain. The cars and trucks and buses all seemed to lose a little paint, gain a little rust and soot; the faces looking out at the passing traffic wore expressions of rage or grief or numb remove.

The *maras* controlled vast sections of the area, manning their *esquinas* as though guarding a perimeter, selling crank and crack in single-hit *papeles* in hand-to-hand buys or through storefronts called *tienditas*. It was one of the reasons the country was falling apart—the cartels paid in product, not cash, and so the *maras* dealt locally, creating a whole new strata of lost souls. Colburn and Satcher, two white strangers in a rented sedan, triggered hand signals from the lookouts on their corners as the car sped past, and though the two men were armed—not just their pistols but short-stock M4s stowed in the trunk, pre-loaded magazines, plenty of rounds, even smoke grenades if needed—it would be far wiser to avoid trouble than fight their way out of it.

Colburn turned down a narrow side street, pulled to the curb and murmured, "We have reached our destination, *el capitan*."

On the sidewalk outside a car repair shop, two satin-lined coffins lay open for display beneath a canvas canopy. Colburn and Satcher greeted the portly, mustachioed *calequero* who sat outside, nursing a cup of coffee, his Stetson nudged up on one side to make room for the cell phone pressed to his ear. A tip from a trusted cop or fireman, Satcher figured, someone with the word on a murder victim lying on the street somewhere. There were the same number of murders here now as Mexico, which had thirteen times the population. Shortly the man would be off, rushing to the scene to get the details, then hustling away to the family with an affordable package that included everything from help with finessing the death certificate to paying off the gravediggers.

Colburn, using Spanish, told the man who—or what, at this point—they were looking for. Never taking the phone from his ear, he waved them inside.

They strolled past the car repair bays and an ancient Coke machine to the rear where, among engine blocks and retread tires, a bone-thin woman who'd tucked her hair beneath a butcher's cap smoked a carefree cigarette, taking a break from her work on the three naked bodies laid out on narrow work-tables. She leaned against an iron sink, her back to a wall of greasy tools, her floral-print dress protected by a filthy apron. Overhead, a fluorescent coil hanging by chains flickered, casting an erratic purplish light. Winchester flagons of alcohol, lanolin, silicone and various dyes lined metal shelves, with discolored tubing and soiled rubber gloves scattered here and there among knives, pliers, saws.

Satcher spotted him right away, one of the three: Pingüe. He was a street-baller for Mara Salvatrucha and, up until now, Satcher's inside source on the movements of one Chepe Salguero, son of Amado Salguero, head of Los Betos, a local franchise of the Sinaloa cartel.

It was a simple division of labor, Colburn taking Lope as his source, gathering the big picture, Satcher's focus more narrow, more specific, working the street for someone with an in, a pipeline to the source. It had taken weeks and no small amount of money, but gradually Pingüe had come on board.

Like most criminal syndicates in the region, Los Betos was largely a family affair, with the *capos* and closest advisors all uncles, cousins, brothers, nephews, which meant not just loyalty but jealousy. Chepe Salguero had fallen out with his father and had set up a side operation, dealing meth and crack locally through gang henchlings like Pingüe. A small betrayal, but betrayal all the same.

Satcher and Colburn had been green-lighted for a snatch and grab, with the assumption that, once transported to a black site, given the proper attitude adjustment and tutorial, aware that even if freed again his father would just finish what these curious strangers had started, Chepe would provide the information on the family business only a trusted insider could. A simple arrest at the hands of the national police or even the DEA wouldn't do. The family, realizing discipline could wait, would close ranks, embrace the prodigal son and hire the best lawyers, threaten the prosecutor, bribe the judge. No, it needed to be handled off the record, which meant a call to Sterling Associates, the entity from whose Cayman Island trust accounts Colburn and Satcher drew their pay.

Satcher had been recruited during his tours in Iraq with the First Marines. He'd realized by the second battle for Fallujah that the secret to survival in war, let alone sanity, lay far above his pay grade. And though he'd prepared himself for the hopeless grief and stern regret of sending men to their deaths, he'd underestimated the disillusion of doing so at the command of distant, fickle, self-congratulating fools. Like a lot of captains and colonels who'd led combat units in that fight, he'd joined the exodus of those who opted for decommission and private hire. Security work, the new *condottieri*, off-the-shelf and off-the-record. If the CIA formed the muscular arms of plausible deniability, men like Satcher and Colburn were its agile fingers. No one could compel them to disclose their clients, and most times they had no clue regardless, lacking any need to know. They received an encrypted email with a location, a target, names of reliable locals and a fee, and were off.

The tactical aspects were left to them, which meant the jobs were routinely better planned than his ops in Iraq had been, no ass-backward ROE's drafted by committee, sent from the Pentagon to cover the collective butt. The work was surgical, though the point was often murky—dirty tricks in a grim world, or however you chose to think about it—and that was the little backdoor through which his disillusion returned. In the end, the same faceless, self-anointed geniuses were calling the shots; the rest of the world existed simply to pick through their trash. He was just a glorified *chacharrero*. But it paid the rent, as they say—condo in Tampa he seldom saw, alimony, child support.

Colburn's path had been similar: deployed to Belfast with the Royal Green Jackets, the Swift and the Bold, walking patrol in West Belfast, tin toby on his head, SA80 in his hands, manning a cordon for a house search with the smoldering stench of peat fires all around as they rummaged out coal bunkers for cast-off weapons or pub bomber kits, scanning the windows and rooftops, wary of snipers or a Provo wannabe in a balaclava with a Molotov cocktail in his fist. From there it was on to Bosnia and Kosovo, but he didn't much like discussing that. "Those people," is all he'd say, "worse than the bog trotters."

Colburn's cell went off and he snatched it from his pocket. "Bloody thing's been banging off all morning."

"If it's Lope," Satcher said, "ask him how he knew my guy was here. That's bothering me, to be honest. You never told him who we had inside Chepe's crew, right?"

Colburn shook his head then ducked back into the service bay to take the call, leaving Satcher alone with the woman and her three corpses.

Pingüe's body focused his mind. They'd spoken at most a handful of times, but bonds get sealed on far less. He'd reminded Satcher of some of the Sunni kids he met in Anbar, surly and cocky, curious and scared. From the look of his wounds he'd been knifed repeatedly, up close work, sign of a gang job, or something meant to look like one. But at that moment it was his tattoos that fascinated Satcher. They were florid and gothic but intricate too, densely interwoven across his chest and face the same way the tiny maniacal arrows in Brandon's drawing locked and meshed together. The Users and the Used. And for all Pingüe's menace and *tigueraje*, his knowledge of weapons and street weight, he and Brandon were roughly the same age. Fourteen, he thought, come September. *Try not to forget this year,* Julia had said.

In lisping Spanish, caused by missing teeth, the woman

explained who the other two were: a bus driver murdered for not providing his weekly tax to the *mareros*, and a security guard killed by vigilantes for groping a nine-year-old girl. The vigilan- tes were more common in the countryside, where the old civil defense patrols linked to the military had killed with abandon throughout the civil war, but they were cropping up here and there in the cities now, too, another sign of the general disor- der. No one trusted the law. Odilia had gone on and on about it. "We're on the verge of civil war again," she'd told Satcher, "except nobody knows which side is which." The military was in bed with the *narcotraficantes*, rogue soldiers and cops ran kidnap and car theft rings, judges and prosecutors were corrupt or com- plicit, even the vigilantes themselves were suspect, as *mareros* or other gangsters posing as concerned citizens used the killings as a way to even scores, eliminate rivals.

As for Pingüe, the woman explained that his body was found that morning in a garbage-strewn ravine outside the capital. The family didn't have the money for burial and his *clica* refused to pitch in because of rumors the boy had been a *dedo*, a snitch. She said this as she stubbed out her smoke, watching Satcher closely. He responded that if Pingüe's killers had truly thought he was an informant, they would have cut off his fingers and stuffed them in his mouth, but he knew that wasn't the point. She was hoping he was DEA, the boy's handler, and out of decency or guilt would pitch in to cover the cost of his embalming.

Colburn stuck his head in from the service bay. "Satch—a word outside?"

Back on the sidewalk, he gestured Satcher into the car, then drove two blocks before saying anything. "This doesn't get bet- ter, regrettably."

"Lope?"

"No, sadly. Not a peep from him. It was a friend I've cultivated, an FSO at the embassy. He just got word that the national police are raiding the Salguero *finca* in Asunción Mita today. As we speak, actually. Caught the DEA flatfooted, they had no clue. And the word is the whole bloody clan is there—the PNC got a tip from a local."

"The whole clan—you mean Chepe's out there too?" The prodigal. The target.

Colburn nodded. "So goes the word. What say we trek out to the countryside, have ourselves a look?"

Satcher sank into his seat, gazing out at the misty haze, the decaying tamped-down *barrio*. If the PNC, the national police, were involved in the raid and hadn't bothered to alert the Americans, it could only mean one thing. "We're too late."

"Now, now." Colburn found his way back onto 7 Avenida, heading for the Panamerican Highway. "Pessimism, surest mark of an amateur."

"They're going to arrest them together, Chepe and his old man. It's a stunt. The PNC's in on it with Papá Amado. Christ, the OC directorate's just another gang."

"No doubt of that, but maybe we'll catch some luck."

"Listen to me, we've been made. The mission's been blown. What did Lope say exactly when he called you this morning?"

Colburn waved him off. "Pretty extreme, wouldn't you say? The PNC and Los Betos get together and cook up a scheme to give the whole Salguero clan up to the law, just to keep the faithless son from the old bag-and-gag?"

"Given the damage Chepe could do if we're the ones who get to him first?"

"Why not just kill him?"

"They're buying themselves protection, throwing the government a bone. The PNC can claim a major coup, parade everybody in front of the cameras, *el jefe* will make a speech. Then day by day, week by week, bribe by bribe, the thing disappears. Meanwhile they've got time to badger Chepe back into the fold."

Colburn frowned. "Seems like a lot of moving parts."

"The way the courts work down here?" Satcher thought again of Odilia, remembering her shyness as she'd dressed, slipping back into her virtue. "Jail's just a way to regroup. And with the connections Old Man Salguero has? They'll get cells that look like condos—TV, Internet, everything but a French maid. Plus plenty of time for a father-son heart-to-heart before the charges get dropped. It'll happen, trust me."

Colburn sighed lavishly. "No doubt the whole thing's gone tit's up. But we can't just jack it in without so much as a look now, can we."

THEY DROVE OUT TO the easterly edge of the country to Asunción Mita, a rustic, mid-sized town in the hills, reaching it mid-afternoon. Satcher's mind drifted as the car sped along the curving, two-lane highway. Try as he might to stay focused on Chepe Salguero, the chance to somehow salvage the job, bribe him away from the PNC maybe, bustle him off to the safe house they had ready in the capital, his thoughts invariably turned to his son, Brandon, the hopeless behavior, the inescapable trouble and deepening isolation—was there blame to be had in that? Was there a way, as a father, to escape blame? He wondered what Odilia would make of that, imagining she'd come down solidly on the side of loyalty, children, family. Blame. Strange, how he was seeing everything now, from the outer landscape to his inner life, through her eyes. He'd spent a single night with the woman but something had turned, something he had no right to. She'd loathe him if the true nature of why he was here spilled out. Too much like Cold War dirty tricks and death squads, the kind of thing she was dedicated to ridding from this country, her country, for good.

Normally, he just considered such qualms foolish, but that was because the naysayers knew nothing, their ignorance was their sole claim to virtue, a virtue easily dismissed as preciousness and hand-wringing. Odilia was different. She was the sexy equivalent of nuns he'd met—steely, calm, down-to-earth, risking their lives to do a simple good thing. Clothe the poor. Nurse the sick. Demand justice. She's the hero in this, he thought, imagining what she might say: *You're no better than they are.* But was it necessary to be better? Wasn't smarter and stronger and more disciplined enough? History wasn't written by the better, after all, just the ones left standing. And the parts left out never happened.

Colburn found a café and pulled to the curb. "I got a number from my pal at the embassy, local bloke, one of us more or less, knows we're coming. Let's ring him up, see if he'll grace us with a chat." He flipped open his cell, thumbed the number, got through, said simply "We're in town" and gave the name of the café, listened for a bit, then "Right" and hung up. To Satcher: "Might take a while, they're up to their chins, but he said he'd come round as quick as he could. Nothing to do but wait, I suppose. Late lunch sound about right?"

They ordered *churrasco* with *frijoles parados con arroz*, scooped their portions with fresh *tortillas* and chased it all with weak coffee braced with sugar. Satcher hadn't realized how hungry he was; sated now, he felt half-inclined to let his head drop to his chest, catnap in his chair. Instead, he drew on his near Olympian skill at waiting, professional requirement for soldiers everywhere, picked up a newspaper for camouflage, pretended to read. It was well after dark before their contact appeared.

His name was Falk and, in this part of the country, he served as the DEA's chief liaison with the national police. It made him both trusted and tainted, like everyone else they dealt with. He looked about the room before sitting down.

"One thing's clear before we start," he said quietly. "I'm not here. Neither are you."

Satcher glanced about the room as well—mostly women, a few men, clerks and ranch hands from the look of them, but that meant nothing. "Shall we drive?"

"Head back toward the capital, same way you came. About a half mile outside town, you'll see a cemetery, big pillared entrance painted red. Gate'll be open, drive in, park, walk along the leftmost path. Careful, it's dark out there."

With that, Falk left, and Satcher and Colburn waited another five minutes before following. Once on the road they checked for trail cars, spotted none, and shortly pulled up at the cemetery, parked beyond the big red gateway Falk had described, the paint blistered, the plaster scarred, the entrance to a forgotten sepulchre. The tombs near the front were elaborate if neglected, little citadels awaiting their mourners, with ironwork fences and statues of kneeling virgins and crucified Christs, deeply shadowed by moonlit *ceibas*. Gravel crunched beneath their feet as they followed the path Falk had described, glancing everywhere for strange young men, cemeteries being favorite hangouts for *mareros*. None appeared. They caught the groan of trucks making the hill behind them on the highway, otherwise silence.

Falk waited midway back, finishing a cigarette that he crushed into the gravel as they approached.

"You guys scared the crap out of somebody," he began. "I don't know who found out about you or how, but this thing was quite a show. Nobody's going to think it wasn't real."

Colburn and Satcher glanced at each other. Satcher said merely, "Interesting," to which Colburn added, "You mean to say you're not going to kick up a fuss, make people aware the national police staged a raid against a major cartel and you were damn near last to know?"

"Not the way things work," Falk said, trying for stoic, sounding beaten. "Not down here. You know that."

"Sorry, mate, I meant no—"

"It's all about relationships, right? Cooperation. Which means learning to smile when you're lied to. Besides, they'll just say they were acting on a tip, had to move pronto."

Maybe it was the cemetery, or the sudden caw of a *zanate* high in the branches of one of the *ceibas*, or everything Falk wasn't saying, but Satcher felt something turn a little further inside him, a click. Next time he saw Odilia, he'd tell her about this, tell her everything.

"Mind filling us in," he said. "How it went down, I mean."

"They raided the *finca* this morning at daybreak," Falk said, "broke into a warehouse and found, I'm not kidding, something like eight thousand drums of phenylacetic acid, acetone, ephedrine, you name it, some of it from Paraguay, some from China. Worth maybe a couple tons of crystal. PNC had a camera crew on hand, of course, and the *jefe* bragged about shutting down the biggest meth super lab—"

"They had time to call the media," Satcher said, "but not you."

Falk shrugged, waved a dismissing hand: Forget about it.

"Meanwhile, every villager who can stand upright is crowding the edges of the scene. This foreman steps up, moaning about how everybody's gonna lose their jobs. Señor Salguero is their *patrón*. There was nothing but shabby little plots of corn and beans around before he opened his *finca*, they grow coffee and melons and tobacco now—never mind the fucking lab, or the airstrip on the back end of the plantation—did I mention that? Salgueros built the local clinic, the school, the *mercado,* gave a scholarship to one kid to go to the seminary, I'm not making that up. This foreman, he says you close things down, you'll be pitching five hundred people—not just men but women, kids, whole families—to the wolves. Government's a rumor here, the church can't help. If it weren't for Salguero most of them would have emigrated to the States. Christ, Salguero *is* the government here. Without him they starve."

Satcher remembered what Odilia had said about civil war. These weren't gangsters, they were warlords. "Anybody else step up," he asked. "Besides the foreman, I mean."

Falk just stared. "That's a joke, right? Nobody saw *nada.* They're simple people, farming folk. Salt of the fucking earth."

"They're scared. The Salgueros are using the whole damn community as a human shield."

Falk chuckled miserably. "We'll be running a counterinsurgency here before long."

"And you Yanks are so bloody great at that." Colburn, veteran of Ulster, couldn't help grinning.

Falk rummaged in his pocket for another smoke. "You're not gonna start that crap, I hope. I'm doing you a huge fucking favor here."

Colburn grinned and tsked and turned to Satcher. "Touchy."

Satcher said, "What about Salguero himself?"

"The old man?"

"Him, sure. Though, to be honest, I'm a little more interested in Chepe, the son."

"Yeah, well, sorry to be the messenger, but I've got some bad news. Look, I don't know who hired you, I'm assuming the Company." Satcher lifted a nay-saying hand and Falk waved him off. "Yeah, yeah. I get it. But you've got a leak. This whole thing was a hoax. Showtime."

"You've said that." Satcher, infected with Colburn's derision, tried not to sound tetchy. "Look, we heard the thing happened because the PNC got a tip the whole family was here, on the *finca*. That's why they had to move so quick."

"So goes the story, yeah. Except the whole family was long gone before the thing went down. Everybody but Chepe, that is."

Satcher felt his stomach drop. "Chepe was there."

"Manner of speaking. By the time I arrived they'd already taken the body away. He was in the warehouse with, oh what shall we call it, the evidence? Opened up, nine mil, or that's how it's gonna get told. Officers on the scene returned fire."

Everyone was quiet for a moment. The *zanate* in the *ceiba* cawed again. Then Colburn couldn't help himself any longer, he laughed. "Fucking brilliant."

"A little theater for the folks watching at home," Falk agreed.

"Bloody fucking hell." Colburn turned to Satcher. "You see it, right? PNC gets to plant the bloody flag, show off 8,000 drums of seized chemicals, in exchange for killing the turncoat son. As the mistress said to the gardener, quid pro quo."

"Give them a couple weeks," Falk added, "they'll probably turn around and sell the whole haul right back. Talk about win-win."

At the whim of some freak turn of memory, Satcher suddenly recalled teaching Brandon how to ride his bike, holding onto the back fender, hearing the boy yelp over his shoulder, *Don't let go.* "You're saying Amado Salguero arranged with the PNC to wax his own kid."

Falk started heading for the cemetery entrance. "Like I said, you've got a leak. And the family must've figured that, if somebody'd go to all the trouble to send you two down here to snatch their boy, hole him up someplace, work him, then they had to get real about how weak he was. Christ, who knew that better than they did?"

THEY WERE DRIVING BACK toward the capital, the road between villages winding and dark and all but empty. Six months earlier, on this same stretch of highway, *mareros* had burned alive fifteen Nicaraguans and a Dutch backpacker in a bus the killers suspected of carrying a cocaine shipment for a rival gang. Only the over-motivated drove at night. Both men kept alert.

Finally, Satcher said, "Remind me, you got referred to Lope how?"

Colburn sighed. "Usual channels. The man behind the curtain, Daddy Warbucks. Call him what you like."

"You're not going to tell me."

"I've been ordered."

Satcher was floored. "By who?"

"He's one of us, right? Leave it at that."

"One of us. Gotta love the sound of that."

"The man's no saint but he can be trusted, so I was told. "He'll prove useful, just play him close.' Something along those lines."

"Play him close. Meaning keep me in the dark."

"You're not going to whinge about my walking point on this."

"I'm not blaming you. I'm blaming whoever—"

"Satch, bloody hell, what difference does it make? I got my orders, sorry they froze you out, but take that up with the home office, right? And when you do, be my guest, tell them you were right, the thing blew up, a cunting bag of wank. Meanwhile let's go back, grab our bags and passports, *vámonos.*"

Satcher remembered Odilia close beside him in the rain, both of them laughing as they ran, shoes soaked through, the canopy of her blazer over their heads. "Yeah. Let's blow town. Lickety-tickety-split."

"For fuck all—what's gotten you so bloody browned off?"

"Know what I think happened? We're here to kidnap a guy. Not just some guy, Chepe Salguero, as plum a target as they get. Lope and his crew, they think, Hey, that's our racket. So they figured they'd do the snatch, play us off the family, start the bidding at what, a million? Two?"

A slow-moving tanker rumbled ahead; Colburn flashed his brights to signal he wanted to pass. "I didn't tell him about your boy, Pingüe, if that's where you're heading with this."

Satcher looked out as they surged past the truck, the driver refusing so much as a sidelong glance, rigid with fear. "I told you, I'm not pointing fingers. Christ, it's probably my fault. I got tailed to a meet, they saw Pingüe, figured him for our link to Chepe, decided to pay the kid a visit themselves."

Colburn glanced at his mirror at the slow truck vanishing behind them. "He's a good actor, I'll grant him that. Lope, I mean. This morning, my wake-up call. He didn't sound coy or false, far from it—"

"They snatched him up, Pingüe, tuned him hard, too hard. He didn't know where Chepe holed up when he came to the city, we were working on that, but Lope's not the kind to believe it. He's the kind to think that a little more pain should do the trick. That or something else went haywire, it's the only way this makes sense. So he's got a dead *marero* on his hands and moves to Plan B, calls Old Man Salguero, tips him off to our plan, lets him know we came here to turn his feckless boy against him. Figures that's worth something down the road."

Colburn murmured, "All about building relationships—or however our man Falk put it."

Outside the window, moonlit hills looked down on valleys dense with shadow, the small tin-roofed *champas* along the road dark and still except for the occasional barking dog. Satcher said, "Don't you ever get weary, being the last to know?"

"You mean ignorance isn't bliss?" Colburn tapped his thumbs against the steering wheel. "Someone should tell my dear mother."

"I'm serious."

Colburn took a moment to suggest an appropriate degree of reflection. "Seems a silly kind of question, frankly, coming from a soldier."

"I thought this would be different."

"It is. The pay's better."

"They knew." Satcher couldn't get it off his mind: *The man killed his own son.* "The geniuses at the home office, your man behind the curtain, whoever the hell dreamed this up, they knew all along."

"Now now, let's not get manic."

"Somebody made a counter-offer, changed sides. If not Lope

153

then somebody. A wink, the secret handshake, a suitcase full of money. Wonder when they were going to bother to fill us in."

"I'm serious, mate, where you're heading? Ice doesn't get thinner." They began to see headlights, a bit of oncoming traffic; Culiapa was coming near. "Our job's to bag up villains, not pick winners, leave all that to finer minds. Meanwhile, as I said once before, cynicism's the true mark of an amateur."

Satcher studied the man's profile in the dash light. Sharp features, all angles and planes, cavernous eyes. He wore no band, never mentioned a wife, seemed indifferent to children; if they existed, he put them far from mind. Satcher remembered Julia, his ex, saying at one point during the divorce, *If only half the man I'd married had come back from that war.* He recalled Odilia, the reformer, the hero, stepping forward to say goodbye, an ingénue kiss. Imagined Brandon bent over his drawings—*time to get real about how weak he is*—pictured him with a bullet in his brain.

"Pessimism," he said finally.

Colburn slowed the car as they entered the town proper. "Excuse me?"

"Before, it was pessimism you said was the mark of an amateur. Not cynicism."

Colburn glanced out at the low dark buildings lining the road: bakery, tire repair, evangelical church. "Distinction without a difference, mate."

SATCHER FEIGNED SLEEP the rest of the drive, inwardly plotting the way out. When he returned to his room he'd email the home office, tender his resignation. Then sleep, if he could. Come tomorrow he'd ring Odilia, ask her to lunch, come clean about who he was, deal with that. Maybe he'd tell her about

Brandon, put all his regrets on the table, pony up the whole sorry state of his conscience. Maybe they'd talk about the difference between romance and redemption. He'd let her know he was willing to join the team, go after the Lopes and Amado Salgueros in her country, not in the shadows but the light, like her. Maybe his skill set would put him in good stead, maybe not. Maybe his history would do him in. If worse came to worst, someone in her circle no doubt needed protection—a lot of the prosecutors were young, with families, death threats came in daily. One way or another, he'd put himself to use. He needed some clarity. He needed fewer lies.

Near midnight, as they reached the edge of the capital, his cell went off. "Here we go," he said, figuring now they'd learn the truth, or what would pass for the truth. Digging the phone from his pocket, he checked the display, expecting the call was from one of the clones used by the home office, but the number wasn't one he recognized.

He flipped his cell open, waited. Nothing. Then a shrill voice, barking through static and chaotic noise: "¿Quién es?"

On a hunch, Satcher lied: "No hablo español. Ingles, por favor." Shortly he heard murmuring away from the phone amid the clamor, then a new voice, deeper, calmer, still heavily accented, the superior he'd secretly hoped for: "Hello. I am Inspector Domingo Palma. Who is this, please?"

Twenty minutes later they were at the scene, the crowd held back by uniformed cops, strobe lights swirling, the dizzy beams of light caroming off the walls and windows of nearby apartments. Inspector Palma—bearish man, worry bags under the eyes, unlit cigar—shook Satcher's hand, grunted like a surly barber, then produced from his pocket a slip of hotel stationary. Satcher recognized it instantly, even before he saw his cell num-

DAVID CORBETT

ber scrawled on it. *I should be here another week.* He glanced at the paper fleetingly then looked past the inspector to the bullet-riddled car where she slumped forward, gory with blood and suspended in her shoulder harness like a marionette hung up for the night. The windshield was all but gone, just a shattered maw of jagged glass, white with fissures.

"We think she pull over," Inspector Palma said, "for call you."

Satcher nodded, wondering if the man could be trusted, or if he was a member of Lope's crew, assuming it mattered now. *No one knows which side is which* ... Staring past him to the car, he could see she was wearing a different blouse than the one she'd had on that morning. Of course, he thought, no self-respecting young professional would be caught dead, as it were, traipsing about in the same clothes she'd worn the night before. He felt Colburn's hand on his arm, shook it off, while remembering her standing alone, clutching her champagne flute at the embassy. *I should not have drink so much.*

"Tell me, Mr. Satcher," Inspector Palma said, pronouncing the name *sad chair*, "do you have here, how to say, *enemigos?*"

The voice seemed to come from a thousand miles away. Satcher was focused instead on the ground around the car. Hundreds of brass shell casings littered the asphalt. They'd used machine guns: Overkill. A little theater for the folks watching at home, as Falk would say. The casings pointed every possible direction, cast about in odd random symmetries, suggesting both an impossible confusion and an invisible center of gravity.

All rights reserved under International and Pan-American Copyright Conventions. By payment of the required fees, you have been granted the non-exclusive, non-transferable right to access and read the text of this book. No part of this text may be reproduced, transmitted, downloaded, decompiled, reverse engineered, or stored in or introduced into any information storage and retrieval system, in any form or by any means, whether electronic or mechanical, now known or hereinafter invented, without the express written permission of the publisher.

This is a work of fiction. Names, characters, places, and incidents either are the product of the author's imagination or are used fictitiously. Any resemblance to actual persons, living or dead, businesses, companies, events, or locales is entirely coincidental. Though the locales mentioned in the narrative exist, many geographical and topographical details have been altered for the sake of the story and dramatic effect. Accordingly, they should be regarded as entirely fictitious.

"Pretty Little Parasite" (2008) first appeared in *Las Vegas Noir* by Akashic Press. "The Axiom of Choice" (2009) first appeared in *Strand Magazine*. "Stray" (2010) first appeared in *The Smoking Poet*. "It Can Happen" first appeared in *San Francisco Noir* by Akashic Press. "Bobby the Prop Buys In" (2005) first appeared in *Meeting Across the River from Bloomsbury*. "Dead by Christmas" (2009) first appeared in *Phoenix Noir* by Akashic Press.

Copyright © 2012 by David Corbett

ISBN: 978-1-4532-6432-4

This edition published in 2012 by MysteriousPress.com/Open Road Integrated Media
180 Varick Street
New York, NY 10014
www.openroadmedia.com

EBOOKS BY DAVID CORBETT

FROM MYSTERIOUSPRESS.COM
AND OPEN ROAD MEDIA

Available wherever ebooks are sold

MYSTERIOUSPRESS.COM

INTEGRATED MEDIA

FIND OUT MORE AT

WWW.MYSTERIOUSPRESS.COM
WWW.OPENROADMEDIA.COM

FOLLOW US:

@eMysteries and Facebook.com/MysteriousPressCom
@openroadmedia and Facebook.com/OpenRoadMedia

OPEN ROAD

INTEGRATED MEDIA

Videos, Archival Documents, and New Releases

Sign up for the Open Road Media newsletter and get news delivered straight to your inbox.

FOLLOW US:
@openroadmedia and
Facebook.com/OpenRoadMedia

SIGN UP NOW at
www.openroadmedia.com/newsletters

www.ingramcontent.com/pod-product-compliance
Lightning Source LLC
Chambersburg PA
CBHW030510260626
47157CB00005B/1731